Other Works by B. Heather Mantler
The King's Ransom
For Wealth and Glory

Committed to Her Enemy

# Closing the Portal

B. Heather Mantler

Mantler Publishing Prince George

ISBN:1927507022
ISBN-13:9781927507025
**Library and Archives Canada Cataloguing in
Publication**
**Mantler, B. Heather, 1987-      Closing the portal / B.
Heather Mantler.**

**ISBN 978-1-927507-02-5**

   **I. Title.**

**PS8626.A676C56 2012      C813'.6    C2012-907072-6**

For Mom, Weston McGee, Howard Karpes, Chris Rempel, and Ian. Your help has been invaluable to me.

# NARDA WANTS TO BE TREATED LIKE AN ADULT AND GETS IN TROUBLE BECAUSE OF IT

Narda sat on a bench in the garden staring at the yellow flower she had found growing in a crack between paving stones. The gardeners had not been out tending to the beds recently, otherwise they would have pulled the flower out. It was not a particularly pretty flower, but Narda remembered reading about it in one of her books. She could not remember what the name of the flower was. She did remember that it was considered a weed, but the greens were edible and the flowers could be made into wine. However, it was rare for people to do either with it. Most of those flowers had been eradicated from the kingdom of Proster, but there were still some places where they could be found. Narda knew that if the gardeners found it that they would pull it up and then burn it. It was the best way of making sure that the seeds did not spread.

"Narda," her mother's voice called. It sounded like her mother was near the door to the castle.

Narda slowly got to her feet. She started back along the path that would lead her to the door, but she walked slowly as if the speed would change what awaited her at the end of the path.

It did not. Her mother was standing there with her hands on her hips and an expression of impatience on her face. Her brown hair was braided back out of her face and her pink gown had golden trim which matched her necklace and earrings.

"If you do not hurry, you will make us all late for church." Ruana looked her daughter over. "You still need to get dressed."

"I do not want to go to church." Narda said, "Father does not go to church."

"Your father worships in his own way," Ruana said as she pushed Narda into the castle, "and you may worship in whatever manner you wish once you are grown up."

"I am grown up." Narda said, "I am fourteen. Sherine is the same age and is betrothed."

"What happens under Lord Redmond's roof is his business." Ruana said, "You live under this roof and as such you are to follow the rules. That means you are to get dressed this instant. You are coming to church."

Narda allowed herself to be pushed inside and down the hallway. When they reached the bottom of the stairs, Ruana pushed Narda to go, but did not go up with her. Narda went up the stairs and into her chambers. Her new maid was waiting for her with one of the dresses Narda wore to church set out on the bed along with all the necessary accessories. Narda gave in and allowed herself be dressed in the outfit.

Once Narda was dressed and ready the maid left the room. Narda looked at herself in the mirror. The dress was a blue silk with lots of lace attached. The matching blue shoes were uncomfortable to move in. And her brown hair was braided and wrapped around her head in a way that Narda thought made her look like a child. Narda stuck her tongue out at her reflection before turning to the door. She left the room.

Her father was coming down the hallway when she stepped out of her room. He was wearing the brown and grey gambeson he wore to sword practice. He would put on the rest of his armour when he reached the castle armoury.

"And here is my delightful daughter." Proster smiled, "How are you this morning, Princess Nava?"

Proster stopped to give Narda a hug. She was six inches shorter than he was and Proster kept saying that she would be taller than he was in a year if not sooner. She had her mother's height, but many of her father's personality traits.

"Why do I have go to church?" Narda asked, "I do not want to go. You do not go."

"You have to go because your mother wants you to go," Proster answered, "and we humour her."

"Why?" Narda asked.

"Because she is your mother and you should obey her." Proster said, "In two years, you will be all grown up and then you do not have to go."

"That is too long," Narda said, "I do not want to go today."

"And why do you not want to go to church?" Proster asked.

"There is a man that sits behind me." Narda answered, "He spends the whole service staring at me and I find it creepy. I told mother and she just said that he was not used to sitting so close to royalty, but he has been doing it for months. I tried sitting somewhere else, but Mother just demands that I sit with her. He does not bother anyone else. And since he has not done anything besides stare so Mother will not listen to me about him anymore."

"Go today," Proster said, "and if he is still there and still staring I will talk to your mother about the problem."

"Okay," Narda's tone said that she was not happy, but she knew that was the only answer she would get on the subject for now.

Before Proster could tell Narda to hurry up, Herwin came up the stairs with a serious look on his face. Herwin wore a grey, velvet doublet which matched his hair and black hose with shiny black shoes.

"Proster," Herwin said, "there is a problem."

Narda stopped and stayed where she was; the last time that Herwin had said that it had been a threat against the whole family and they had to stay home from church. Proster continued to where Herwin was. Herwin told Proster what was going on in a hushed tone. Narda made out the words trouble, demon, and threat. Proster nodded to all this and responded, but Narda could not hear what he said. Herwin turned and went downstairs. Proster turned back to Narda. He smiled at her.

"You better hurry," Proster said, "or your mother is going to be upset with you for making her late."

"Yes, Father," Narda said. She was disappointed, but

went down the stairs.

Narda did not argue with her father, because he never said anything unless he truly meant it. That was probably why he was such a popular king for one who had taken the kingdom of Proster by force.

Her mother was waiting for her near the door that led to the courtyard. Narda joined her and they went out to where the carriage was waiting for them. Narda's brother, Zebulon, and sister, Hertha, were already inside. Narda sat down in the seat across from them and her mother slid in beside her.

No one spoke for the ride to the church. Both Zebulon and Hertha were lost in their own thoughts and Ruana was looking out the window. Narda stared down at her hands.

The carriage stopped just as Narda realized that she had forgotten her gloves. There was nothing she could do about that now. The door to the carriage opened and Ruana was helped out by a footman. Zebulon followed his mother out before turning to help Hertha down. Narda followed Hertha out, ignoring the offer of help down. Ruana headed up the stairs and into the church with Zebulon and Hertha close to her. Narda was just about to follow them when she saw her friend Parisa. Parisa was on the edge of the crowd as she begged for change so that she could buy something to eat. The people going passed ignored her. Narda glanced at her mother and siblings. They had not checked to see if she was following them. Narda went over to Parisa was. Parisa looked surprised to see her.

Parisa was shorter than Narda by almost a foot with delicate features. Her eyes were a soft brown and her ears had a slight point at the top. Her light brown hair hung to a little below her chin. Narda was not quite sure how old Parisa was, but Parisa had not changed much in the time she had known her. Parisa also did not know who her parents were; her only memories were of the orphanage where she had been left as a baby. Since no one had adopted her Parisa had been left to fend for herself. Which was why she was dressed in a dirty shirt with several holes in it, dirty pants, and shoes that she picked out of someone else's garbage.

Narda had met Parisa a couple years ago when Narda had snuck out of the castle because her mother would not let her go shopping in the marketplace alone. Narda wandered the marketplace for hours looking at all the fascinating stuff that was for sale. She had not bought anything because she could not find exactly what she wanted. She had seen Parisa begging near a stall and the owner of the stall telling her to go away. Narda decided to help Parisa, but before she could one of the city's guard arrived to run Parisa off. Parisa had looked pitiful as she stood there in rags and was just looking for food. Narda had stepped in and asked the guard to leave Parisa alone. Parisa had not been sure about accepting Narda's help until Narda bought food for Parisa. They had been friends since and Narda would give Parisa food or money for food whenever they were in the marketplace.

"Narda, what are you doing here?" Parisa asked.

"My mother demanded that I come to church." Narda answered, "I am here every Sunday."

"I would have thought that you would be kept home with what has been happening," Parisa said.

"What is happening?" Narda tilted her head to the left.

"People have been going missing for the last week." Parisa answered, "The first was an eight-year-old baker's son, then there was the ten-year-old blacksmith's daughter, and the twelve-year-old nobleman's son. Word is that someone is going to disappear tomorrow. There are warnings to stay off the streets and avoid the market place. I am out here begging because I won't get anything tomorrow."

"I had not heard about any of that," Narda said.

"Maybe they think that you are protected from all of this." Parisa said, "You do have a lot more guards around up there at the castle."

The number of people going into the church decreased as the last of them arrived for the service.

"I should go in," Narda said.

"I will have to try somewhere else," Parisa said.

"Want to join me?" Narda gestured toward the church, "I will give you some money."

"I have never been inside of a church before," Parisa said.

"As long as you are quiet it is not too bad," Narda said.

"Sure, I will come with you," Parisa said.

Narda headed into the church with Parisa following her. Inside the church, Narda led the way to a staircase that was to the right of the door. They went up. This staircase came out on a balcony. There were a few other children already up there, peering through the railing at the service below. Narda and Parisa got down on their hands and knees and crawled to the railing, where they lay down on their stomach and looked through the railing.

The priest was already at the front. He was starting

into the first prayer. Narda looked to her mother's usual pew near the front of the church. She was seated there with Zebulon and Hertha beside her. Even from a distance Narda could see that her mother was not happy, but was ignoring the problem of Narda's absence to concentrate on the service.

Her mother had always been more religious than her father. Her father spent an hour or two a week mediating and praying. Her mother never missed church if she could help it and she prayed several times a day. Her mother worshipped God and her father worshipped Saint Ingram. Narda believed that there was one god out there, but she also figured that there were saints working to help people, which her mother did not agree with. Her mother never said anything about that to her father, of course, because he believed. It was one of only a handful of things that they did not agree on.

Narda looked over the congregation as the priest went through the beginning prayer. She noticed that a lot of people had their children with them. That was unusual as most children were allowed to run around and did not have to sit with their parents. She even saw that her friend, Laken, was sitting between his mother and his father. He looked very uncomfortable and squirmed in his seat. He would glance behind him and around at the rest of the people. Laken glanced up at the balcony. Narda waved. Laken looked at his mother and then his father, before giving up and trying to concentrate on the priest at the front.

Something was happening and no one at the castle was talking about it. Either that or word had just reached the castle that morning. She had not overheard anything to do with missing children. Maybe the missing children had to do with Herwin talking to her father about the demon. That would make some sense. At that thought, Narda looked at the pew behind where her mother was sitting. The man who was creepy was not sitting there. She looked over the congregation for him, but could not see him anywhere. She glanced around the balcony, but there were no adults up there.

The priest moved on to singing a couple of hymns. The congregation stood up to sing. All the children on the balcony remained where they were. Every time an adult found out that they were up here they forced to sit in the pews below for a month until the stairs were no longer guarded again. No one liked that. Narda only managed to get up here when she could escape her mother on the way into the church and if the balcony was guarded she would have to sit with her mother anyway.

Once they songs were over, the priest said another prayer. The he started into the sermon. Before he finished the first sentence, all the children who had been on the floor by the rails had moved back to the far wall. A group of boys started a card game, where they nudged each other rather than talked. Several others took out books and started reading. Parisa moved back with Narda.

"Where did you hear about the missing people?" Narda whispered to Parisa

"Yesterday," Parisa said, "in the market place. Two of the guards were talking about it. But there have been children going missing for about three months. All of them down near the wall, so it is not likely that anyone would care, or look into it."

"Is that was what happened to that woman you were

talking about?" Narda said, "The one who was demanding that the guards return her child."

"Yes," Parisa said, "the guards took her to the convent to see if they could put her mind at peace. Her boy was three years old and he just disappeared one night. There are more children that have disappeared, but no one has been looking for them except their parents."

"That is wrong." Narda said, "My father says that children are the most important part of the kingdom. Why would someone not be looking into the disappearances?"

"The guards do nothing," Parisa said, "and the one time that someone went to the castle no one there did anything to help either."

"I will have to take this to my father." Narda said, "He needs to know what is going on. He will do something about it."

Proster paced in front of the dais as Herwin and Garrick stood there with Loic, who was the captain of the guard.

"You are telling me that there are several children missing and you have no clue to what happened to them." Proster said, "They were put to bed and were missing when the parents woke up."

"Baker Morris's son, Clint, Blacksmith Barson's daughter, Iris, and Lord Hervay's son, Oriel, have all gone missing in the last week." Garrick said, "I visited each place afterward and there were no clues on where the child went. The parents report that the doors were locked and no windows had been opened during the night. Whoever did this made sure that they did not leave any trace."

"It is more than that." Loic said, "There have been reports from the area closest to the city wall of children going missing for the last two or three months."

"Why has there not been any word of this until now?" Proster turned to face Loic.

"I did not hear about until I joined a patrol going through the area two days ago." Loic answered, "The men that patrol that area have ignored the people's cries for help with the situation. I have since put them on duty of a less pleasant sort. Then more children disappeared and I had to check that out."

"Any clues from those disappearances?" Proster asked as he started pacing again.

"Many of the places do not have doors let alone locks." Loic answered, "So, anyone could have taken the children without many obstacles. The youngest child that has been taken is three months and the oldest is Oriel."

"Find the parents of the first child to disappear." Proster said, "Bring them to me. I want to talk to them."

"Do you think they will have answers?" Herwin asked.

"I do not know," Proster answered, "but it is a good place to start. In the meantime, we need to be gathering all the information we can."

"Should we alert the people to what is happening?" Loic asked.

"As little as possible." Proster answered, "Some will already know that something is going on and will need to be told that we are doing the best that we can. If a person does not know we do not want to panic them. Panic will make it harder for us to figure this out."

"Yes, sir," Loic said. He left the throne room.

"You two, visit every place you can where a child has disappeared." Proster stopped to look at Herwin and Garrick, "You will come back here and tell me if there is anything strange or unusual about the house, the household, and that such."

"And what will you do?" Herwin asked.

"Sit here and think." Proster answered, "Something is strange about all of this and I keep getting the feeling that I should know what it is."

"Okay." Herwin said, "We will be back with the information you requested as soon as possible."

Herwin and Garrick left the throne room. Proster went back to pacing.

The priest had finished his sermon and was leading the final song. All the children on the balcony crawled back to look through the railing for the song after putting away what they had been using to entertain themselves. Once the song was over, the priest went into the final prayer. And finally the service was over. People started to stand up and head for the exits. Narda saw her mother and siblings not move from the pew, which was usual since her mother preferred to wait until most of the crowd had cleared. Her mother was searching the crowd with her eyes trying to spot Narda.

Narda and Parisa crawled away from the railing with the rest of the children. Narda and Parisa waited as the rest of the children went to the stairway before going down them. At the bottom, Narda and Parisa left the church. Narda looked for Laken. She finally spotted him, but he was still with his parents, who were hustling him into a carriage. Narda was disappointed that she did not get to speak to him. Parisa looked like she wanted to get away from the crowd. Narda led the way to the edge of the crowd and down beside the stairs to the church.

Narda was thinking about giving Parisa the money that she had promised so that Parisa could go home and eat, when she saw the man that sat behind her every Sunday. He was standing between buildings across the street from the church. He was wearing dark clothing. And today his eyes were glowing red. Narda felt her blood run cold and fear froze her in place. But the man was not looking at her, he was looking at the carriage with Laken and his family in it.

"What is it?" Parisa asked.

"Him," Narda nodded to the man in the alley.

"I have never seen him before." Parisa said, "Who is he?"

"I do not know," Narda answered, "but I have a bad feeling about him."

The carriage went by and the man stepped out of the alley. He started to follow it.

"Come on," Narda pulled off her shoes before starting to follow the man.

"Where are we going?" Parisa asked as she trotted after Narda.

"To find out where he is going," Narda answered.

"This does not sound like a good idea." Parisa said, "He could be dangerous."

"Then we will try not to let him know that we are following him," Narda said.

"Okay," Parisa did not sound sure, but she went along with Narda.

Proster had stopped pacing and was sitting on the throne when the door to the throne room opened again. Loic stepped inside followed by a woman. The woman's clothing looked like it came from a poor box ten years ago and her face was streaked with dirt. Her brown hair was braided back with loose pieces framing her face.

"Sire, this is the mother of the first child to have gone missing," Loic announced before bowing. Then Loic took a step back so that the woman was closer to the dais. The woman curtsied before looking up at Proster. She was trying to control nervousness as well as holding back tears.

"Your name?" Proster asked.

"Chelle," the woman answered.

"Your child went missing?" Proster asked.

"My son, Ansel, was taken from me." Chelle said, "No one has believed me about it. Do you believe me?"

"Yes, I do." Proster answered, "How long ago was Ansel taken from you?"

"Two and a half months," Chelle answered.

"Was there anything unusual happening at the time?" Proster asked.

"I did not notice anything," Chelle answered, "but I was caring for Ansel and trying to keep myself fed. Ansel was only three months old when he was taken. Are you going to get him back to me?"

"I am just trying to figure out what is going on." Proster said, "Though I hope that Ansel can be found and brought back to you."

"Thank you," Chelle said.

"Do you remember anything about that night that could help?" Proster asked.

"I had laid Ansel down after feeding him." Chelle answered, "I was to sleep near him. Before I was asleep I thought I heard footsteps, but they sounded far away. Then I fell asleep and did not wake up until morning. I got up and went to check on Ansel and found that he was gone. That is all I remember. Does that help you at all?"

"A little bit." Proster answered, "Loic will escort you out and as soon as I know something about where Ansel is I will send a message to you."

"Thank you," Chelle curtsied again before allowing herself to be led out of the throne room.

Proster stood up and started pacing again. There was an alarm ringing in his head, but no answer to why he should be so alarmed.

Narda stopped beside a fence and ducked down so that she would not be seen. Parisa crouched down beside her. The carriage was outside of Laken's house. Obviously the family had just gone inside and the driver had not moved the carriage. The man had stopped in front of a store that was on the other side of the street. Narda and Parisa were hiding behind a fence two buildings down where there was a tee intersection with another street.

"What is he going to do now?" Parisa whispered to Narda.

"I am not sure." Narda whispered back, "I think he might be after Laken."

"You mean that he is the one kidnapping people?" Parisa asked.

"I think so," Narda answered.

"But all the rest were taken during the night." Parisa

said, "It is only noon."

"Laken's parents go visiting in the afternoons." Narda said, "The servants are usually allowed to whatever they want on Sunday afternoons. If Laken is not visiting someone then he is at home in his room. It is easier to get him on a Sunday afternoon then it is the get him at night when the house is heavily guarded."

"So, we watch and see if the man goes after Laken." Parisa said, "When what? What if he does take Laken? What do we do?"

"I do not know yet." Narda said, "I am still trying to figure that out."

"We should find a guard," Parisa said.

"We cannot do that," Narda said, "because we have no proof of anything and the man might disappear if we leave. The guard is more likely to take you back to the orphanage and me back to the castle. If I go back to the castle, then I am going to have to listen to the lecture on running off on my mother, as if I am just a child. It is better if we had some proof before going to the guard."

"Okay." Parisa said, "But we cannot fight the man on our own, if that is your thought."

"I am not foolish." Narda said, "We would likely go missing along with the rest of them and then we would be in worse trouble. No, we are just going to watch him and see what he does."

"Okay," Parisa said.

Proster was pacing back and forth in front of the dais, while Loic sat in a chair he had dragged over from the table that sat on one side of the room.

"I do not remember anything like this before." Loic said, "There were lots of different kinds of demons, but

I do not remember one that kidnapped children. Most of them are flasher than that. This activity seems too hidden. There is a chance that Lord Hervay's guard saw something he did not understand and assumed that it was a demon."

"Lord Hervay's guard claimed to see the man's eyes glow red and Oriel under one arm." Proster said, "He also spent some years around here fighting things that came out of the portal. He knows more about demons and pixies than anyone else around."

"Did he know what type of demon it was?" Loic asked.

"We might be able to ask him if he ever wakes up." Proster answered, "He was found badly beaten. They got a full sentence out of him before he lost consciousness. He said that Oriel was kidnapped by a demon. That is how we know as much as we do."

"But it could just be a man, who has learned magic by being too close to the portal," Loic said.

"It could be." Proster said, "That is why I am looking for so much information. Then we will be able to figure out."

"What did talking to Chelle get you?" Loic asked.

"That was someone there," Proster answered, "and the person probably put her to sleep."

"How long until Herwin and Garrick return?" Loic asked.

"A while." Proster said, "I will need you to coordinate the guards. Two on every street and the city locked down. They are all to do what they have to do to keep this city safe."

"Yes, sir," Loic replied.

The door to the throne room opened and Ruana

stepped inside. Proster stopped pacing to look at her. The joy of seeing his wife bloomed in Proster's chest. He almost smiled at her, but her expression stopped him. She was worried and frustrated.

"What is wrong?" Proster asked.

"Your daughter is missing." Ruana answered, "She did not follow us into the church and we were just about late so I could not go looking for her. After the service, we waited for her to show up as she usually will. She did not show up and I have no idea where she is. I asked a few people, but none of them had seen her."

"We will find her," Proster said, "or she will turn up. She knows that supper is her favourite foods. She will show up then, if she does not show up before then."

"I know," Ruana said, "but I am tired of her disappearing on me. Zebulon grew out of all that by the time he was fourteen and Hertha never went off on her own like that. We need to find something that will keep Narda busy and out of trouble."

"I will talk to her about it as soon as she turns up," Proster said.

"Did you try and talk her into going to church?" Ruana asked.

"I did." Proster answered, "She told me that she did not want to go because of a man that sat behind her. She found him creepy."

"She has said as much," Ruana said, "but I have not noticed anyone back there."

"So, you did not notice if he was there today?" Proster asked.

"There was no one back there today." Ruana answered, "I was looking around for Narda when I could and there was no one back there."

"We will talk about it later then," Proster said.

"What happened?" Ruana asked looking from Proster to Loic and back to Proster.

"A demon is at work in the kingdom," Proster answered, "and we are trying to figure out what we can about him so that we can hunt him down and get rid of him."

"That is awful." Ruana said, "I hope you all the good luck you need to find this demon and dispose of him."

"We will do what we can." Proster said, "Do no worry about it. Go out and doing your usual visiting." Ruana nodded before she turned and left the throne room.

"We need all the luck we can get," Loic muttered as Proster started to pace again.

The smell of roast chicken was coming from one of the houses and Parisa's stomach growled.

"Can we find some food?" Parisa asked.

"In a few minutes," Narda answered, "I do not want to be somewhere else when he makes his move."

Parisa shifted a little to get more comfortable.

"Here comes Laken's parents," Narda said. Parisa looked over and saw the couple come out of the house. They went down the stairs and into the carriage. Once the carriage pulled away several of the servants left the house. Laken did not come out.

A minute went past as Narda and Parisa watched the man stand there. Finally the man looked both direction and then crossed the street. He went up the steps and disappeared into the house.

"He is going after Laken." Parisa said tugging on

Narda's sleeve, "What are we going to do now?"

"Wait for them to come out and then follow them," Narda answered.

They crouched there for five more minutes before the man came out. When he came out he was carrying a brown sack over his shoulder. He went the opposite direction from where the girls were hiding.

"He has Laken in the sack," Parisa said.

"Let us go," Narda said.

Narda and Parisa straighten up and followed the man.

He went down through the streets. They left the higher class houses behind. He went through the streets where the shop keepers lived and had their shops. And then he went through the streets where the poor lived. Finally he reached the gate to the city. Narda and Parisa stopped at the gate and stood watching him as he went along the road. He headed down the road to the left.

"Should we keep following him?" Parisa asked when Narda did not take a step outside the city.

"I know where he is going," Narda said, "and we are going to need a few things before we go after him."

"Should we tell someone about this?" Parisa asked.

"We can handle this." Narda answered, "Come on."

Narda started back up the street the way they had come. Parisa stayed where she was. Narda turned back when she noticed that Parisa was not following her.

"What is it?" Narda asked.

"I am hungry," Parisa answered, "and I never got enough change to buy food."

"I have money." Narda said, "We can buy something on our way."

"Okay," Parisa caught up to Narda and they started

moving again.

Proster sat on the throne as Herwin and Garrick repeated to him everything they had gathered so far, which amounted to nothing. If he had not asked for it, Proster might have told them to stop. The most they had brought him was a list of the children who were missing, their ages, and when they disappeared. He read it over, while listening with half an ear for any useful piece of information that might come from his advisors. The names on the list meant nothing to him, but that was not a surprise since he did not interact with the people to whom the children belonged to. The dates they disappeared meant nothing to him either. It was regular intervals, but nothing special that stood out about the dates. However, the ages were surprising. The youngest was Ansel at three months and each child was a little bit older than that as they were taken until it came to Oriel, who was twelve. The information brought something to mind.

"I know what we are dealing with," Proster interrupted Garrick. Garrick fell silent and both looked at him expectantly.

"I remember looking up this kind of demon." Proster said, "It is known as a collector, because it collects things. It picks something to collect and then it collects that starting at the smallest and working its way to the biggest. They do not tend to be dangerous unless cornered and if they cannot get the item they are collecting then they will come back another time."

"This one is collecting children?" Herwin asked, "That does not sound like to collector."

"A collector is usually a messenger for another

demon." Proster said, "Very rarely do you find one working on its own. Whoever this collector is working for probably wants children for something and he is gathering some for his private collection."

"What is he doing with them?" Garrick asked.

"I do not know," Proster answered, "but we need to find him and get the children home."

"Where do we start?" Herwin asked.

Before Proster could answer the door to the throne room opened and Loic stepped inside.

"Yes, Loic?" Proster asked.

"Ruana asked me if I would see if I could find any trace of Narda." Loic answered, "I went to the church and looked around. I found Narda's shoes beside the steps of the church, but there is no other trace of her."

"Narda is missing?" Garrick asked.

"After complaining about not wanting to go to church, Narda did not follow Ruana inside," Proster said, "and she has not been seen since."

"I cannot find any trace of her besides her shoes," Loic said.

"She will show up for supper." Herwin said, "She would not want to miss her favourite foods."

The three men looked at Proster, whose eyes had lost focus and a wrinkle of concern appeared on his forehead.

"Proster?" Herwin said.

Proster shook his head to clear and focused on them again.

"Narda did not want to go to church because the man behind her was creepy." Proster said, "Ruana did not notice the man. The collector is kidnapping children for something that wants children and Narda is the right age to be the next on his list."

"I will take a handful of guards and one of the dogs." Loic said, "We will see if we can pick up her trail."

Loic left the throne at a pace close to a run. Proster was up off his throne and down off the dais before Herwin and Garrick could react.

"Where are you going?" Herwin said as they hurried to follow him.

"I am going to get my sword and armour," Proster answered, "and meet the demon at the portal. The portal is the only place he could be taking the children. You two get your weapons and armour and anyone else that you can round up to fight. We are going to take this fight to the demon's battlefield."

"Yes, sir," Garrick said before he and Herwin ran off to obey his commands.

Proster took the stairs as fast as he could without running. He would have a servant take a message to Ruana to explain what was happening since she and Hertha were off visiting for the afternoon. Zebulon would be reading in the library, but Proster had never found him to be useful while welding a weapon of any sort. He was much better with words and knowledge. Fortunately, he also had the brains to use them in a way that would befit a king.

Proster opened the door to his bedroom and headed straight to the closet. He pulled out the useful pieces of armour and started to put them on. When he was had his armour on, Proster left the room and headed down the stairs to his study.

In the study, Proster pulled back the bookcase that had hidden the Wizard Slayer for years. Proster rarely had taken it out because he had very little use for it and he worried that someone might try to steal it. Occasionally he would take it out and made sure that it was still sharp and ready for use, but otherwise it was hidden behind the book shelf. He had opened it up just yesterday and made sure that it was battle ready. Proster looked into the cache and was shocked to find it empty. He stared at the space for a minute before feeling around and checking the space. The Wizard Slayer was gone.

Proster shut the cache and checked over his office, but the sword was nowhere in sight. Proster growled in frustration, he was going to do a thorough search for his sword later. He grabbed one of the swords he had been given as a present when he was crowned king. The other three were useless decorative trash, but this was a sword made for battle. He usually used it for occasions when he had to wear a sword. Now he was going to have to take it into an actual battle.

Sword in hand, Proster headed for the stable to get his horse.

Narda kicked the horse into a gallop. They had lost more time than she had wanted when they stopped in the market place to buy lunch and found that most of the food vendors had packed up already and gone home, or had not come out for the day. They had to go all the way up to the castle and get some food from the castle kitchens. Parisa had been awed by how big the castle was and by all the food that was prepared in the kitchen. For the first time in her life she had eaten until she was full and then had been given more to take with her. Narda had changed out of the awful dress and into clothing more suitable for following the man. She had also found some clothing for Parisa as well. Then Narda had done something that was going to get her in a lot of trouble if her father found out. She took the Wizard Slayer from his study.

Narda knew what the sword meant to her father, but if she was going to come face to face with a man whose eyes glowed red she was in need of a weapon. She had brought her bow and arrow as well, but she did not think that they were enough, especially if she ended up in close combat with the man. She had found a short sword for Parisa. When Parisa had picked it the sword looked full sized, but it was a short sword. Parisa was not sure about taking it, but Narda assured her that it was not anyone's sword and that it was okay for her to use it. Parisa was not quite sure how to use it, but Narda figured that she would do okay.

So they were armed and had some provisions as they rode the horse that Narda had borrowed through the streets of the city. No one bothered them, or got in their way because there were only a few people out in the street to see them go passed. Everyone seemed to be scared that if they wandered the streets they too would go missing. Narda thought that was foolish, but her father had explained to her many times that people were not the most sensible of beings, especially in large groups.

The horse finally reached the gate and Narda directed him along the path that went to the left. Then she spurted him into a run. Parisa held on to Narda tighter as they started to go faster. They left behind the city walls with in minutes and headed into the forest.

Herwin, Garrick and Loic had gathered as many men

as they could find in a short amount of time. Half of the guard was there and several of the noblemen were gathered when Proster came out into the courtyard. He mounted his horse before turning to the group, all of whom were already mounted.

"We are going after the demon that has been stealing children from the city." Proster told them, "I thank you all for coming to help me with this." Several heads nodded, but no one spoke. They all knew the basics of what they were up against and were more than willing to follow Proster.

Proster had his horse start forward, but did not get farther than that before he saw another horse riding up. Vila came riding into the court yard and over to where Proster had stopped. Vila was out of breath and it took a moment before he could speak. Proster waited patiently, while the men behind him shuffled a bit.

"My son is missing." Vila finally gasped out, "We went out and when we got back we found that he was gone. None of the servants saw anything. But he did not take anything with him that would suggest that he left of his own will."

"We are leaving to go in search of a collector demon that has been kidnapping children." Proster said, "We will see if we can find him."

"Thank you," Vila nodded to Proster. Vila moved out of the way. Proster started forward again and the rest followed.

They had just left the court yard and were moving into the city streets when Herwin moved up to ride beside Proster.

"Two children in one day." Herwin said, "That is a strange thing for him to do unless he is suddenly in a hurry."

"I spoke with one of the cooks as well as a few other servants." Proster said, "Narda received some food from the cook. She was also seen near her room. It seems to me that she likely kicked off the shoes before going wherever. The cook also mentioned that she had another girl with her."

"So, she is not a worry for the moment." Herwin said, "That is good."

"No, I fear that she is in great danger." Proster said, "She took food with her, as well as her bow with arrows, and she borrowed a horse a full half an hour before I reached the stable. Whatever she is doing is not likely to be safe if she is arming herself."

"What should we do?" Herwin asked.

"Keep an eye out for her," Proster answered, "and pray that she does not get into too much trouble before we can find her."

Herwin nodded and dropped back as they continued through the streets of the city to the city gate.

# THE MAGICAL PORTAL AND WHAT IS INSIDE

They had been going through the forest for half an hour when Narda directed the horse off the path and into the brush. The horse slowed down to a walk, because it could not run with the amount of brush.

"How close are we?" Parisa asked from behind Narda.

"An hour," Narda answered.

"I have not seen any signs of the man who took Laken," Parisa said.

"He is headed for a portal that is in these woods." Narda said, "I have seen the portal's location on a map, but I have never seen it for real."

"Then how do you know that the man went to the portal?" Parisa asked.

"Because that is the only place that makes sense for someone whose eyes glow red," Narda answered.

"You did not tell me his eyes glowed red." Parisa

said, "You did not say anything about a portal either. Maybe we should go back and tell someone what we saw."

"We would be in too much trouble if we go back now," Narda said, "but if we bring back more than just guesses we will not be in as much trouble."

"I am not sure about this." Parisa said, "The man could be dangerous."

"We will be fine," Narda said.

Parisa was silent, but she still had the look of disapproval on her face. Narda ignored it.

Fifteen minutes of riding the horse through brush brought Narda and Parisa into part of the forest where the horse could not go because the brush was taller and thicker. Narda and Parisa climbed down from the horse and started into the brush. Narda left the horse's reins on the saddle horn just in case they were not back before it got hungry.

With each step Narda and Parisa were raked with branches on both sides, up to their knees in brush, and could not see passed the next bush. But they kept going. There were several points where they crawled because there was no other way to get through.

Both Narda and Parisa were tired and thirst when they finally stumbled out of the bush and into a clearing. Once free of the branches, both girls sat down on the soft grass of the clearing. Narda pulled out the water skin she had brought for herself and took a drink. Parisa waited until she had caught her breath before doing the same.

Narda looked around the clearing. It was a perfect circle with not so much as a branch within that circle. Grass grew in the clearing, but there were no wild flowers, or other plants. In the exact center of the clearing was the portal. It was eight feet high, five feet wide and constantly swirling making it appear to have depth. The swirls were silver and blue. It felt like if you stared it too long it would hypnotize you.

"The man is not here." Parisa said, "There are no traces of him. Should we wait for him?"

"No, we should not wait for him." Narda replied, "He is in there already. I doubt that he had to walk through that brush. He is in there and we are going to go get him."

"We are going into the portal?" Parisa said, "Is that not dangerous?"

"That is why we have weapons," Narda replied, "but I think we need to rest and maybe have a snack before trying this."

"Okay," Parisa said. She took out the bag that the cook had given her. She offered some to Narda before taking some for herself.

They did not speak as they sat there in the grass and ate. The portal continued as it was and nothing came out of it for the length of time that the girls sat there. When the food was all eaten, Parisa put the bag away, but neither of them moved.

"It was a cloudy day this morning," Parisa looked up at the sky.

Narda looked and saw a cloudless sky with sunshine.

"I guess it could be different out here." Parisa said, "I remember thinking about not going to the market place today because it could rain. Now it is cleared up."

"I do not think that the weather in this clearing has anything to do with the weather in the city," Narda said, "or even the rest of the forest."

"I noticed the circle, but I did not think it would affect the weather as well as the trees," Parisa said.

"Magic is a powerful force that most people do not understand." Narda said, "I know little pieces because my father told about them or from reading about them. That much information is the same as finding a seed in a forest."

"A portal is made up of magic." Parisa said, "If you do not know much about magic and I know nothing about magic, is it really a good idea for us to follow the man inside?"

"If you want to stay here, you can," Narda said, "but I am going in to find the man." Narda got to her feet and gathered her bow and quiver of arrows from where they had fallen when she stumbled out of the trees.

"I am coming." Parisa said, "I am just not sure that this is a good idea." Parisa also stood up, but she was slower moving in gathering everything.

When both had everything with them Narda and Parisa took several steps toward the portal. They stopped just short of it.

"Do you feel the pull?" Parisa said, her voice was hushed. Narda glanced at Parisa and saw that she was staring into the portal.

"No," Narda shook her head. Parisa took her eyes off the portal to look at Narda.

"It is pulling me," Parisa said.

"Let us hold hands." Narda held hers out to Parisa, "Then we will not get separated."

"Okay," Parisa said taking Narda's hand.

The two girls stepped into the portal. The swirling of colours continued as they both felt like they were suddenly falling. After a minute they hit a solid surface and everything was black.

"Who are you?" a male voice growled from somewhere in the blackness.

"We are looking for someone." Narda answered, "He went in here and he had a friend of ours with him."

"But who are you?" the voice repeated.

"I am Nava," Narda said, "and this is Parmida."

"Hmm." Narda felt like she and Parisa were being studied.

"A human and a fairy." the voice said, "A strange combination."

"A fairy?" Parisa asked, "You must have that wrong. I am human."

"Raised among human most likely," the voice said, "but most definitely a fairy."

"Then how come I do not have wings?" Parisa asked, "Every fairy in every story has wings."

"I do not know, child." the voice was scolding, "Perhaps living among humans as had its detrimental effects on you. I do not know everything about fairies, I am just the guardian of this portal."

"We need to find the person who has our friend," Narda said.

"Patience, child." the voice said, "I am the one who will decide whether or not you will be allowed to enter."

"I am not a child." Narda got to her feet, "I am old enough to take care of myself and old enough to fight for myself. Your ignorance and insults will not stop me from my objective."

"Really?" the voice was amused by something, which made Narda angry. She wrapped her hand around the hilt of her father's sword.

"Well, since nothing will stop you, I guess I have to let you through." the voice said, "Good luck on your quest."

"Narda!" Parisa's voice held a note of warning, but before she got the word all the way out the blackness was gone and they were falling again.

This time it was a short distance into a pit. Narda was the first one to her feet and dusting herself off. She helped Parisa up. The sun was shining down into the pit so Narda could see most of the dirt bottom and sides, but there was an edge of darkness where the sides met the bottom. The sky was light blue and there were no signs of anything above the sides, not even trees. There were no people up there to help them out either.

"We are in trouble." Parisa said in a quiet voice as she looked around, "He did not just let us in without doing something that would amuse him."

"Aside from the fact that we are in a pit, I do not see anything," Narda said.

A growl came from behind them. This one was deeper than the guardian's had been, but more menacing. The girls slowly turned around and looked behind them. Slinking out of the darkness that was along the walls of the pit was a hellcat. It had the body of a panther, but it had scales instead of fur. There was a natural collar of denser scales protecting the neck. The yellow eyes had black slits for irises. The hellcat opened its mouth to roar at the girls and showed off a mouth full of white teeth that looked very sharp.

Narda drew her father's sword and Parisa drew the short sword. Then they heard the other two growls from behind them. Narda checked and saw two more hellcats coming out of the shadows.

"This is what he was laughing over." Narda said, "Do you see any way out of this pit?"

"No." Parisa answered as she moved to be back to back with Narda, "What do we do now?"

"The only thing we can do." Narda answered, "We fight until we figure out some way out of here and can run."

"These are hellcats." Parisa said, "You cannot run from hellcats."

"How do you know?" Narda asked.

"I remember someone telling me about them." Parisa answered, "They latch on to your scent and attack until you are dead. They can also jump out of this pit without any trouble."

"Well, then if we want to live through this, we need to kill these three hellcats," Narda said.

"Is that even possible?" Parisa asked.

"I do not know," Narda answered.

The first hellcat jumped toward Narda. Narda swung the sword. The sword slashed the hellcat's side. The hellcat backed away out of the reach of the sword. It licked the wound and Narda watched the wound heal up.

"Did this person who told you about hellcats mention their healing abilities?" Narda asked.

"No," Parisa answered.

"This is going to be a lot harder than I thought," Narda said. The hellcat snarled at Narda and then all three of them attacked the two girls. Narda started swinging the sword. The Wizard Slayer was a long sword and kept the hellcats at a distance from Narda even if her swings were inefficient. Parisa on the other hand was having trouble because she was thrusting the short sword and hoping to pierce the scales without getting scratched.

Narda swung at the hellcats again and again. She was never quite sure if she actually hit the hellcats, but they could not get close to her due to the erratic swings. The sword was heavy and even with two hands she had trouble controlling it. She would aim for the hellcat, maybe scratch it before the sword would land in the dirt and she would have to hoist it up again. It was tiring and she was quickly sweating and out of breath.

Parisa had an easier time thrusting with the short sword. It was of a good weight for her to use. She could accurately aim for a hellcat and hit it, but it did not do much damage because the short sword did not penetrate deep enough to get passed the scales. She spent lots of time dodging the swipes of the hellcat's claws.

"I do not think this is working." Parisa said, "I am not hurting them at all."

"I do not know what else to do," Narda puffed.

"Use your bow." Parisa said, "You are better with that."

"I could try," Narda said. She took another swing with the sword to get the hellcats to back away before dropping the sword in the dirt. She pulled out her bow and had an arrow fitted into it by the time the hellcat was close enough to reach Narda. Narda shot the arrow straight into the hellcat's eye. The hellcat scratched Narda's arm before staggering back away from the fight. Narda did not have any chance to look at the wound before she had to reach for the next arrow. She fitted it into the bow as the hellcat backed away and considered its next attack. Narda shot the arrow and it went into the hellcat's neck just above the collar. The hellcats screeched as it backed farther away from Narda. Narda started to lower the bow when she saw the first hellcat get back on its feet. It had managed to pull the arrow out of its eye, but the eye had not healed up. Narda notched another arrow into her bow and watched the hellcat for its next move. It paced back and forth a few times watching Narda, looking for a good place to attack. Narda shot the arrow at the body of the hellcat. It hit the scales on the stomach and bounced off. Narda quickly reached for another arrow as the hellcat launched itself at Narda. Narda dropped to her knees and let the hellcat go right over her. Then she managed to grab an arrow and fit it into the bow. She shot the arrow at the hellcat's head as it was turning back around to face Narda after landing. The arrow landed between the hellcat's eyes and went through the scales. The hellcat collapsed.

Parisa was still dodging attacks and thrusting the short sword at the hellcat, but the cat just kept on coming. It was forcing Parisa backwards with each attack. Parisa took another step backwards and fell over the sword that Narda had dropped in the dirt. The hellcat lunged at Parisa. Parisa dropped the short sword and picked up the Wizard Slayer. She braced it against the ground with the point toward the hellcat. Already fully into the lunge the hellcat could not avoid the sword. The sword went through the hellcat's chest and came out the back. The hellcat's body landed on Parisa and trapped her there.

Narda notched another arrow in her bow and searched the darkness for the third hellcat. She could not see it and Parisa was making too much noise trying to wiggle out from under the body of the other hellcat.

"Shhh," Narda said. Parisa went still and it was quiet in the pit. Narda turned around as she listened, but she could not hear anything.

"Where did it go?" Narda whispered. Parisa tried to look around, but she was could not move that far.

Narda stayed still for a minute, barely breathing and aware of everything. She could not get any bearing on where the hellcat was.

"Maybe you killed it," Parisa said.

"It was still moving after I put an arrow in its neck." Narda said, "It should be around somewhere."

"The arrow might not have killed it right away," Parisa said. She again started to wiggle out from under the hellcat's body. Narda stayed still another few seconds before going over to Parisa. She put her bow and arrow away before pushing the hellcat to one side. It slid off Parisa and on to its side. Parisa got up before turning back to the hellcat. She pulled out the sword. She turned back to Narda and had opened her mouth to say something when she saw the hellcat lunge at them.

"Narda," Parisa said. Narda grabbed the sword before turning around to face the hellcat. She swung the sword with all her might. It connected with the hellcat's neck and went straight through. Parisa dodged to one side and Narda dodged to the other. They both avoided being crushed under the weight of the hellcat.

Narda picked herself up and dusted herself off.

"Are you okay?" Narda called to Parisa.

"Yes," Parisa answered. She stood up and Narda could see her over the hellcat. Parisa had some black blood from one of the hellcats on her, but was otherwise unhurt.

"Good," Narda said.

"Did you get hurt?" Parisa asked as she came around the body of the hellcat.

"Just a scratch." Narda answered holding up her arm to look at it, "Do you know if hellcat's claws are poisonous?"

"I did believe they are not," Parisa answered, "but I did not know that for sure."

"Let us find a way out of this pit." Narda said, "We will find out if the claws are poisonous in a while and if they are I would rather be out of this pit."

Narda and Parisa started looking at the walls trying to find any way out of the pit. They searched all the way around the pit, but they could not find any way out. Finally they sat down to try and think of a way out. They sat without speaking for several minutes.

"Why did you give the guardian fake names?" Parisa asked breaking the silence.

"I do not know." Narda answered, "It just seemed right. Besides Nava is not a fake name. My father calls me that all the time."

"It seemed right?" Parisa asked, "As in gut instinct that tells you when something is not safe?"

"How did you know about hellcats?" Narda asked.

"I do not remember." Parisa answered, "It was like the information just came into my head when I saw the hellcats. It was like I had known it once, but forgotten it."

"Maybe you have been through the portal before but your memory was altered to prevent you from remembering it," Narda said.

"The guardian said that I was a fairy," Parisa said, "but as far as I know I am as human as you."

"My father had dwarf in him." Narda said, "So, I

have dwarf blood in me."

"All of the fairies that I have heard of had wings," Parisa said, "and I have heard lots of stories about fairies. The grounds keeper at the orphanage liked to tell stories about fairies. He was a little weird, but harmless. There were suggestions that he had been dropped on his head as a child and because of that he had never really matured, but I think he might have actually met some fairies."

"And they all had wings?" Narda asked.

"Every single one of them," Parisa answered.

"Maybe there is some condition that he did not know about," Narda suggested.

"Maybe to get wings I need a wand," Parisa said.

"I thought that fairies did not use wands," Narda said, "that it was sacrilege or something like that."

"No, fairies use wands." Parisa said, "It helps focus their magic."

"I do not think it would matter where wings are involved," Narda said.

"That is annoying then." Parisa said, "What is the point of being a fairy if you do not have wings?"

"I think I have an idea on how to get out of here," Narda said jumping to her feet.

"What is it?" Parisa asked as she got to her feet.

"First we need to-" Narda started. Before she could finish the darkness descended on her and Parisa. They were once again in the darkness that was like when they first entered the portal.

"You can now look for your friend," the guardian's voice came again.

Suddenly the girls were standing in the middle of a field. Narda and Parisa looked around. The grass in the field was only up to their shins with no visible path. There were trees in the distance on all sides. And the sun was directly overhead without any clouds in the sky.

"Well, he let us in," Narda said, "but there is no sign of the man or Laken. Or anyone else for that matter. We need to figure out which way to go."

"I cannot tell which way north is." Parisa said, "There is nothing that would indict which way is which. If someone did alter my memory there is nothing here to trigger anything."

"Let us just go forward." Narda said, "Maybe when we reach the trees in that direction we will find something that will tell us where we need to go. And if this is another test from the guardian we will find that out too."

"A good as anything else," Parisa said.

The two girls started forward. The field was easy to walk through. The only problem was the sun beating down as if it was trying to punish them for being outside while it was out. Narda and Parisa stopped once to sit down and have a drink from their water skins before going on.

The sun seemed to move with them and it remained overhead even though it took a couple hours before the girls reached the trees. When they did reach the trees they stopped in the shade of the first ones and sat down in the grass to have another drink.

"I think we are headed west," Parisa said, "because the sun is going the same direction."

"Either that or it is following us to torment us." Narda said, "This is inside the portal. I expect it to be different in here than it is in our world."

"I think we just happen to be moving in the same direction as the sun." Parisa said, "I did not think that it has any grievances against us."

"Okay." Narda said, "Now that we know that we are heading west, is there anything in this direction?"

"We will have to keep going and find out," Parisa said.

They put away their water skins before getting up and going into the trees. There was a path through the trees as if people came through the field all the time and reached this point in the trees. The path was large enough for two to three people to walk abreast, but would not be big enough for a wagon. The tree branches were low so that it would be difficult to ride a horse through here.

As they walked along, there were the usual noises one would hear in a forest. Birds chirped and sang in the trees, squirrels and chipmunks scurried in the trees as well, and there were rustlings in the brush on either side of the path that were made by small animals. Occasionally Narda and Parisa would catch sight of a rabbit, or other animal.

Walking in the forest was pleasant. The sunlight filtered down through the branches providing plenty of light, but was not beating down on the girls. The dirt path was easy to walk on and there were no hills. The path went straight for a long time.

It did start to twist and turn so it was harder to see what was ahead. Occasionally strange things could be seen through the tree branches. There was a clearing that Narda thought about stopping in the rest, but Parisa pointed out the ring of mushrooms. They moved along. There were the burned out remains of a hut that were half grown over. At one point Parisa thought she saw a unicorn, but it was gone before she could get a good look at it.

The path started to straighten out a little bit and it was possible to see where they were headed. Ahead were stone spirals just over the horizon that looked like it be might part of a town or something like that. But what caught both Narda's and Parisa's attention was the man walking along the path a ways in front of them. He was the man from the city and he was still carrying a brown sack over his shoulder.

"That's him," Parisa said.

"We have to catch him," Narda said as she picked up her pace. Parisa matched her pace and in a few minutes they were both running after the man.

He did not seem to notice them following him. And they did not seem to be getting any closer to him. In fact he seemed to be getting farther away from them than closer. Both Narda and Parisa quickly ran out of energy to keep running. They slowed back down to a walk and tried to keep him in sight.

He continued along the path as the trees started to thin and the forest receded making way for another field. The stones spirals were getting thicker as more of them could be seen. The castle they were attached to slowly came into sight. Once it was fully in sight then the wall of the city around could be seen. It looked to Narda like the castle was built on a hill with the city surrounding it. There was a large double gate that was in the wall to the city and it was open all the way as if to let visitors inside, but there were no people around. There were no wagons bringing things into the city. There were no people leaving the city. There were no guards at the gate.

The man headed straight into the city. Narda and Parisa hurried to keep him in sight. They reached the city wall and found the gate surprisingly small. The main gate of the city back home was fifteen feet tall and at least that wide. This gate was only about eight feet tall and about seven feet wide.

Inside the city they could no longer see the man and there were no sounds of him moving around the city. There was no noise at all in the city. No people around, no animals around, nothing moving at all. Narda and Parisa stopped and looked around. The buildings were made of stone and wood. It looked like any other city, except that it was built for people who were less than four feet tall. That fit Parisa well, but for the first time in her life Narda felt too big.

"This place gives make me nervous." Parisa said, "Who would build a city and not have people living in it?"

"Maybe the man built it for the children he had gathered to live here," Narda answered.

"The buildings are too short for that." Parisa said, "The children would grow up and become too big for the buildings."

"Let us move on." Narda said, "We need to find out where he went."

They headed up the street they were on. There were mostly shops on this street. All of it looked like it might in Proster, except there were no people. Narda and Parisa reached the first cross street and stopped. Close to one of the buildings were a stone statue, but it did not look like someone anyone would carve on purpose or anyone would buy. The statue was bending down to pick up a basket that was set on the ground. The basket was not made of stone. The statue's skirt probably came to her knees if she was standing straight, but since she was not the skirt had come up so that her underclothes were visible. The statue also had stone wings that looked like they should have fallen off.

"I did not think that is a statue," Parisa said.

"It cannot be a statue." Narda said, "No one could carve such a thing without it breaking. This is probably what happened to the people that lived here."

"It is a fairy city," Parisa said.

"That would explain the height of the buildings," Narda said.

"If I really am a fairy, I would really like to know why I do not have wings," Parisa said.

"Come on." Narda said, "Let us see what else we can find."

Narda started forward again. After a few seconds Parisa followed.

They went straight up the street. It was only about six blocks before they came to the hill the castle was on. There were no buildings near the castle itself because that area was too steep to build on. Narda and Parisa followed the path up the hill to the doors of the castle. There were two stone guards on either side of the door to the castle. The door itself was open as if the last person through it did not care enough to close it. Narda and Parisa went inside. Since this was the castle, the door was seven feet instead of four, so Narda did not have to duck to go inside.

Inside the castle, they immediately stepped into the throne room. The throne room was full of stone statues of fairies. The king had been holding court before all of them had been turned to stone. Narda and Parisa went up the centre of the room to where the king sat. He was also stone, except for the crown on his head. It also seemed to Narda that his eyes moved, though she was not certain of that.

"The spell did not completely work on him," Parisa said.

"But it worked enough that we cannot ask him what happened," Narda said.

"So, what do we do now?" Parisa asked, "We have no idea where the man went with Laken and the fairies have all been turned to stone so they cannot help us."

"We will have to search the city and find out where the man went," Narda said, "and perhaps while we search we can figure out what turned these people into stone. Once they are back to normal they can answer our questions. You can ask them whether you really are a fairy and why you do not have wings."

"Let us get searching." Parisa said, "Should we split up or stay together?"

"Split up." Narda answered, "We will be able to cover more ground that way. But if either of us discovers something we investigate it together."

"Okay." Parisa said, "I will start in the city. I will be in the buildings closest to the bottom of the hill and work my way to the left and out to the wall."

"I will search the castle before starting to the right." Narda said, "Be careful of the statues, we do not want to cause them any harm."

"I will be careful," Parisa said. She turned and left the throne room the way they had come in.

"I am sorry that we cannot ask your permission," Narda told the statue of the king, "but I am afraid that we would not be able to help you if we do not search. I know my father would be upset if someone came in without his permission. I will search in a way that is as respectful as I can." She bowed to the king. He did not move, but she sensed that she was welcome to search the castle.

There were two doors out of the throne room, one of each side of the room. Narda walked over and went through the door that was to the right of the throne. This door led to a hallway that curved around as the outside wall of the castle did. Narda stepped into the hallway and closed the door behind her. She followed the hallway around. There was nothing along the hallway until she came to what must have been the back side of the castle, then there was a door along the left wall. Narda opened it and looked inside. There was a landing directly inside the door which had one set of stairs spiral down and another set of stairs spiral up. There were torches along both sets of stairs that had not burned out and did not look like they would any time soon.

Narda stepped inside and closed the door behind her. She started up the stairs. The stairs spiraled upward for a long time before another landing came. This one had three spiral staircases going up off it. Narda picked one and went up it. At the top of the stairs was a circular room. The view from the window showed Narda that the room was at the top of one of the stone spirals. This room appeared to be a storage room. There were boxes and crates stacked on top of each other and pushed up against the wall where it was possible. It looked like a person could just come in, identify the stack, take out the crate that they wanted, and then put the stack back without moving anything else. But the space in the centre of the room was extremely limited. It would take several days to go through all those crates, but the dust suggested that they had not been touched recently. So, Narda left everything as it was when she entered and went back down the stairs.

She took the next staircase that went up. This one led to another landing like the one she had just left. The landing had three staircases going off it. Narda went up the one to her right. It went up to a single door. She opened it and went inside. This room had shelves along the walls. All the shelves had books on them. Most were not full of books, but rather had several volumes on them. Most of the books looked to be very old with a thick layer of dust on them. There was one book with only a thin layer of dust on the shelf near the door. Narda picked it up and looked at the book. It was titled *Herbs for the Novice Spell Caster*. As interesting as the book looked, Narda put it back on the shelf before leaving the library.

She went back to the landing and up the next set of stairs. This set also stopped at a door. Narda opened the door and stepped inside. This room was the armoury. Sets of armour, as well as weapons of all sorts were put away in proper places along the walls. All of the armour and weapons were the right size for fairies to use them. Narda thought she should bring Parisa back here at some point since she could use this stuff. Then Narda left the room and went back down the stairs.

She went up the third staircase from that landing and came to another landing. This one had four staircases off it. Narda went up the one to her right. This staircase led to a room without a door. In this space were three sets of bunks that consisted of three bunks hanging off the walls. Each bunk had a blanket and a pillow, but there was nothing else. The bunks looked slept in, but there were no personal effects anywhere in the room. Narda did a quick search of this room, but did not find anything that would be useful. She went back down that staircase to the landing.

Narda went up the next staircase. This room was also storage with crates and boxes stacked along the walls. The only difference was that this room did not have a door. Narda went back down the stairs. She went up the next set of stairs. This one led to another door. But this door has a symbol carved into it. Narda did not recognize the symbol, but touched the door with the Wizard Slayer to make sure that it was not protected by magic. There was no shock, or blue flame that would suggest that the door was protected by magic. Narda put the sword away and opened the door.

This room must have belonged to the court magician. There was a bunk on one wall and the rest of the walls had shelves. There were about three tiers of shelves and all of them held glass jars. Inside each jar was an herb, an object, or a piece of something that was once alive. In the middle of the room was a table. On the table were several glass containers, a spell book, some loose herbs, and small caldron on top of a heating element. Narda went to the table and looked at the spell book that was open. It was a spell for getting rid of scars. There was a window over the bunk. Looking out it, Narda figured that this room must be the tallest stone spiral. Which explained the longer set of stairs to reach it. Narda checked the rest of the room, but there was nothing here that she thought could help her. If she knew something about magic she might have thought about taking more, but Narda was too cautious to mess with magic stuff. She left the room and closed the door behind her.

At the landing, Narda went up the last set of stairs. This room also did not have a door. It contained nine bunks in the same manner at the other one with bunks, except that in this one there were no blankets or pillows and there was a thick layer of dust on everything.

Narda went back to the first landing that had three sets of stairs going up and she went up the third one that she had not explored. At the top of this one was a bedroom. There was a bed with a purple velvet bedspread that had gold edging. There were several rugs, most overlapping each other. They were also purple velvet with gold. There was a wardrobe, a vanity, and a fireplace. Narda figured that the bedroom was the king's room. Narda quickly went through the room. She made sure that everything exactly as it was before she went through it.

Narda could not find anything in the king's bedroom so she went back down the stairs to the landing. She went down the staircase that went to the main floor. She reached it without incident.

Narda started down the stairs from the main floor. As she went down there were longer intervals between torches until it got dark between them. Narda stopped and listened. She heard the sound of water coming from below her. It was not the sound of dripping water, but the sound water makes when it is splashing against stone. Narda went down a few more steps, but stopped again. This time it was the sound of metal against metal. Like someone was rattling the bars of a cage.

Narda turned around and went back up the stairs to the main floor. She would come back with Parisa to investigate the dungeon. At the main floor landing, Narda went through the door and back into the hallway. She headed in the direction opposite from the ways she had come. This hallway curved around the building. There were no doors off the hallway until she came to the one that opened into the throne room. She stepped into the throne room and closed the door behind her. Narda thought it was strange that this castle lacked many of the rooms she thought would be necessary for any building. There was no kitchen, no study, and no dining room. Either fairies did not eat or they just did not do meals in the same way humans do meals.

Narda left the throne room through the door that went outside. She headed down the path and into the left part of the city. She would find Parisa and together they would look into what was in the dungeon.

# FINDING COLLECTIONS AND
# SEARCHING FOR THE COLLECTOR

Reaching the street, Narda looked for Parisa, or any signs of her. Narda went down the street without seeing Parisa. She reached the wall around the city and went down the next street. Narda was half way up this street when she heard a sound. She stopped and listened. There was some clicking, like metal on stone, and some rustling, but it did not sound like Parisa. Narda looked around again, but she could not see Parisa. The noises were coming from a street that was to Narda's right. She moved farther up the street so that she could see down the other one, but whatever was making the noises was not in sight. Narda thought about investigating, but she saw something move up the street.

Narda continued up the street toward where she had seen the movement. She finally reached the spot and found it to be a cloth shop. The door was still open, but

Narda could not see anyone inside. Rather than go inside, Narda knocked on the door. Parisa poked her head out of the back room.

"Did you find anything?" Parisa asked as she came out of the back room.

"It sounds like there is something in the dungeon," Narda said, "but I thought it might be better to check it out together. Did you find anything?"

"The people have been statues for about a week." Parisa answered, "That is just based on a couple houses had people eating and the food looked to be that old. Other than that I have not found much. The shops have things that we could use if we knew what we were doing. There is something else."

"The noise coming from down the street?" Narda asked.

"Yes, that." Parisa answered, "I did not check it out, because I was nervous about doing that on my own."

"Let us check it out first," Narda said, "then we can go check out the dungeon."

"Okay," Parisa said. She stepped out of the shop and closed the door. The girls headed down the street together. They reached the cross street and went toward the noise.

Three houses down was another street. The girls went passed the last house and turned on to this street. They found themselves just short of being nose to nose with a dragon. Narda and Parisa went several steps backwards to put distance between them and the dragon. Then Narda stopped while Parisa went a few feet farther.

The dragon sniffled in their direction as if trying to figure out what they were. The dragon was a young dragon. He was about the same height as Narda and was twice as long. He had green scales with the scales on his belly a lighter shade. His claws and tongue were purple. He also had a collar around his neck that was attached to a chain that was anchored into the wall behind the dragon. The chain prevented the dragon from coming any closer to Narda and Parisa. There was no malice intend in his yellow eyes, just curiosity and pain.

"Narda," Parisa was still backing away.

"I do not think he is going to hurt us." Narda said, "It looks like he has been a victim of the man as well."

"So," what are we going to do?" Parisa asked as she stopped.

"We are going to find something to give the dragon to eat." Narda said, "Then we are going to figure out how to free him. Was there any place you looked where we can get some meat?"

The dragon's ear pricked up and he backed down to a sitting position.

"There was a butcher's shop over a block," Parisa said.

"Okay." Narda turned to the dragon, "We will be back in a few minutes."

The dragon nodded. Narda and Parisa went back the way they had come. Parisa led the way to the butcher's shop.

"He seems very intelligent," Narda said.

"Dragons are known for their intelligence." Parisa said, "It just usually shows up more when they are older. I am sure that he will start talking in a couple hundred years."

They went inside the butcher shop. There was a

statue of a man behind the counter and meats of several varieties hanging up in the back room. Most of the meats looked like they were about to fall off the hooks that held them up.

"We are going to have trouble dragging enough meat back to feed the dragon," Parisa said.

"We need to find some way of carrying it," Narda said.

"I have not seen a wagon at all." Parisa said, "No carts either."

"How about using a blanket?" Narda asked.

"I will be right back," Parisa said before leaving the shop.

She came back two minutes later carrying a quilt.

"That is good," Narda said. She helped Parisa spread it out on the floor. Then they put as much meat on it as they could as still be able to move it. When they were finished, they each took two corners and dragged the quilt out of the shop. They went over the block and to the dead end street where the dragon was. They dragged the quilt to where the dragon could reach it and then stepped back. The dragon sniffed the pile of meat before blowing on it with some flames. This lit the quilt on fire as well as cooked the meat a little, but the dragon ignored the flames as he started to eat. He ate chunks of the quilt if it stuck to the meat.

The dragon chewed through the pile of meat in only a few minutes. He slowed down for the last few mouthfuls.

"I think that was the right amount of meat," Narda said once the dragon was finished. The dragon lay down and rested his head as close to Narda as he could. It looked like he was ready to go to sleep.

Narda walked over to the dragon and studied the collar that was around his neck. He did not move when she touched it. Parisa continued to keep her distance. Narda found a lock holding the collar in place. She took out the Wizard Slayer and tapped it with that. The lock remained closed and there were no sparks to suggest that it had any magic. She put the sword away and pulled out a skeleton key. Narda used the skeleton key and the locked clicked open. She took the collar from around the dragon's neck and put it on the ground. The dragon gave Narda a grateful look and then closed his eyes and went to sleep.

Narda and Parisa left the dragon alone and headed back to the castle.

"I hope all our troubles are that easy to take care of," Parisa said.

"I would like that," Narda said.

They did not say much else as they walked to the castle. At the castle, they entered into the throne room. Narda led the way to the door on the left. They went in and around to the door on the far side. Narda opened this door and they went inside. They went down the set of stairs Narda figured led to the dungeon.

Narda and Parisa were quiet as they walked down the stairs. The first while had torches at regular intervals. Then it was like someone took out every other torch. And then it became only every third torch was left. As they were half way through this last section, Narda and Parisa could hear the water and the rattling. They continued. At the bottom of the stairs they found themselves on an open circular area with six hallways branching off in different directions.

The sound of water came from one hallway and the

rattling came from another. Each hallway was lit with three torches each, which was barely enough light to see the metal bars that made up each cage. There was no way to see beyond that standing near the stairs. There was definitely living things in the cages. Narda and Parisa could hear the sounds of breathing and the scuffling of moving around.

"I wonder what he was collecting before he started gathering children," Parisa said.

"You said that the fairies had only been turned into statues for about a week." Narda said, "The man had been kidnapping children for a couple months."

"This is inside a portal." Parisa said, "Time flows differently here than out there."

"Hello?" a female voice called from one of the hallways.

Narda and Parisa followed the sound and it took them to the same hallway as the sound of water was coming from. Going down the hallway, the girls had to pass several doors of metal bars that looked like cages. It was hard to see into the darkness of each cage and the creatures shrank back into the darkness in fear. Halfway down this hallway, was a set of bars that only went part of the way up. It was twice the length of the other cages and it went down deeper into the floor. The cage was a foot short of being filled with water. Sticking out of the water, were the head and shoulders of a woman. She was floating in the water, but the water the too dirty and it was too dark for Narda and Parisa to see anything below the water's surface. The woman had dark red hair and pale blue eyes. She looked at them with curiosity, not malice.

"Who are you?" the woman asked.

"I am Nava," Narda answered, "And this is Parisa. We are here looking for some children that were kidnapped by a man. We followed him to this city and then he disappeared."

"Who are you?" Parisa asked the woman.

"I am Darla." the woman answered, "I was brought here by a demon called the collector. He collects beings. He was bringing us all here, but I think he might have filled the dungeon and started putting his collection other places. I have seen no human children being brought down."

"What are you?" Parisa asked.

"I am a mermaid," Darla said. She brought her fin to the surface just in front of her so that they could see the green fin. Narda and Parisa looked at it in amazement.

"I think the man that you are talking about is the collector," Darla said as her fin disappeared back into the water.

"Could he have turned the population of the whole city into statues?" Narda asked. Darla frowned.

"I do not think so." Darla answered, "He is not powerful in that kind of way. Most likely the person he is working for did that so that he could have some place for his collection. That is one of the best ways to get a collector as a loyal helper."

"There is more than one of those things?" Parisa asked.

"They are a type of demon." Darla answered, "They usually work for someone else, though a few have become powerful enough to work for themselves. Most of their power revolves around being able to get into places and steal something to add it to their collection. They also can travel fast over any terrain and have the strength to carry things no matter how heavy. Some also have ways of making people sleep until the collector wants them awake, this collector appears to have that ability."

"How do we find this collector?" Narda asked.

"The best way to find a collector is to set a trap and hope that he finds you." Darla answered, "It is almost impossible to find one without it wanting to be found."

"How do we find the collection?" Narda asked.

"There are only two ways that I know of to find the collection." Darla answered, "The first is just by searching everywhere that the collection could be. The second is to use a finder spell. But with the spell you need to know one of the pieces of the collection well enough to visualize it in your head."

"Neither of us is good at magic." Narda said, "We are going to have to go back to searching. Are you okay down here while we keep searching? Because I am not sure how to release you."

"For me, you just open the bars and I can climb up." Darla said, "Once on land my fin turns into legs. The rest of the creatures down here can find their own way home if they are let out."

"As long as they can do so without harming the residents," Narda said.

"We do not have keys," Parisa said.

"I have a couple skeleton keys." Narda said, "They might work in the locks." She pulled them out and gave one to Parisa. Parisa took it and started unlocking the cages on the opposite side of the room. Narda started with the lock to Darla's cage. Once it was open, Darla pulled herself up and out of the water. Narda moved on to opening the cages.

As the doors were unlocked the creatures came out of the darkness. They left the cages and headed for the stairs, where they would disappear up them. Narda and Parisa finished that hallway in moments and moved on to the next ones. Narda went right and Parisa went left. Most of the creatures did not give Narda or Parisa a second glance; they just rushed out of there. A few stopped as if to thank them before leaving.

It did not take long before the dungeon was empty. Narda and Parisa went to the stairs again. Darla stood there waiting for them. Her limbs had light green scales on them and her hair hung down to her thighs. Her red hair was thick and wavy. It also hung in such a way that most of her nakedness was covered up.

"I was hoping that I could thank you by helping you find the children," Darla said.

"We are willing to take all the help that we can get." Narda said, "There should be a clothing shop in the city."

"I found one when I was searching," Parisa said.

"Lead the way," Narda said.

Parisa started up the stairs with Narda behind her and Darla following behind. Darla was walking, but it was obvious that she had not used her legs in a long time and was having trouble with it. Parisa and Narda stopped occasionally in going up the stairs to wait for her to catch up to them. When she caught up to them, Darla would give a smile of appreciation before gesturing for them to continue so that she would not have to stop. Finally they reached the top of the stairs. Darla had an easier time of keeping up with Parisa and Narda as they left the castle and started down to the streets of the city.

The clothing shop was on the main street so it was not far to go. The three of them went inside. Narda had to duck and keep her head bent inside. Darla was about five feet two inches and had to bend down to stay in the shop. They all looked through the shop for something that would fit Darla. Finally, Parisa found a dress in the back. It was leaf green with dark green detailing. The arms fit, as did the shoulders and chest, but the dress ended mid-thigh. Darla tugged the hem lightly, but it would not go down any farther. She shrugged. The three left the shop.

Outside the shop, they came face to face with the dragon. He sniffed at Darla before sitting back and smiling at them.

"I think you have a new pet," Parisa said.

"You fed the dragon?" Darla asked.

"Earlier," Narda answered.

"You now have a loyal companion." Darla said, "He will do just about anything for you now."

"I do not suppose you have a name," Narda looked at the dragon. The dragon titled his head to one side and looked at her.

"I think I will call you Ely." Narda said, "And you and I are going to search for the children on the right side of the city from the castle. Parisa and Darla can search the city on the left side, which Parisa started."

"We can meet back to the castle when the sun goes down," Parisa said.

"See you then," Narda said. She started for the first shop of the left of the street. Parisa and Darla headed for the next street, where they would start searching where Parisa left off. Ely followed Narda.

At the first shop along the street, Narda opened the

door and went inside. She ducked under the door frame to enter. Ely shrank in size until he was able to enter without causing any damage. He sniffed around while Narda poked around. Ely did not alert Narda to anything and she could not see anything. They left the shop, closed the door behind them, and moved on to the next shop.

They went down the first street of shops doing the same thing in each. Narda would look and Ely would sniff for anything. They moved on to the next street and did the same thing. They turned up nothing on that street either. So, they proceeded to the next one. This continued for several more streets. They had finished about a quarter of the city on the right side of the city when Narda came out of a shop and noticed that it was starting to get dark. She and Ely headed back to the castle. As they walked Ely went back to his normal size.

They arrived at the entrance to the castle to find that Parisa and Darla were already there.

"We did not find anything," Narda said, "How did you do?"

"Nothing." Parisa answered, "There was not even traces that anyone had been through any of the buildings in the last week."

Narda sat down in the grassy area beside the path leading to the castle. Parisa and Darla sat down in the grass as well. Ely lied down nearby.

"What do we do now?" Parisa asked.

"We will need to find somewhere to sleep for tonight," Narda answered.

"The collector will be back in our world collecting more children." Parisa said, "We need to find him and stop him."

"I know," Narda said, "but I am tired and it is difficult to search when it is dark."

"To combat the darkness we could take a couple of the torches from inside the castle." Darla said, "They would light the way for us to keep searching."

"I am more worried than tired," Parisa said.

"I am not tired at all," Darla said.

Ely snorted out a puff of smoke. It sounded a bit like he was tired rather than not tired.

"Okay." Narda said, "You two keep searching. I am going to sleep for a while. Ely can stay with me."

"That will work," Parisa said.

"Also while you are looking, see if you can find a way to turn these people back to their normal selves rather than statues," Narda said.

"We will," Parisa said. She and Darla got to their feet and headed inside the castle. Narda pulled out a couple strips of dried meat. She started eating one piece and gave the other piece to Ely. Ely took it and chewed it slowly as if he knew that this was the only food that he would get for tonight. Narda chewed hers.

She had finished the meat and was thinking about searching for a blanket when Parisa and Darla came out of the castle. Darla was carrying two torches and Parisa was carrying a blanket.

"This is one of the blankets from the guard's room," Parisa said offering it to Narda.

"Thank you," Narda said as she took the blanket from Parisa. She unfolded it and wrapped it around herself as Parisa and Darla headed down the path. Narda lay down in the grass with the blanket wrapped around her and closed her eyes. She was too tired to worry about being comfortable. She drifted off to sleep.

Parisa and Darla went back to the shop where they had been last searching before noticing that it was getting dark. Now it was almost completely dark with just one last streak of light on the horizon. The torches did light the way and showed the nearest objects as for what they were, but it made the ones that were farther away seem imposing and strange. The statues of the people took on a more sinister look as the light faded and the torches became the only source of light. And the fact that the statues were already in places that a person might be standing did not help matters.

The shop they had finished searching before going back to the castle had been a blacksmith shop. The next building was a stable. Parisa and Darla went inside. There were ponies inside instead of horses, but they had all been turned to stones, just as their owner had been.

"As least they do not need looking after until we can figure out how to change their owners back," Parisa commented seeing the ponies.

"It looks like the spell was cast on the city and then the collector moved in," Darla said.

"Is that normal?" Parisa asked.

"I have never heard of a collector using an entire city for his collections." Darla answered, "Usually if a being has that much power they did not need help from a demon like a collector. They would get help from a more powerful demon."

"Maybe this being has just enough power to cast the spell to turn all the residents of the city into stone, but not enough to control a demon more powerful than a collector," Parisa said.

"That is possible," Darla said.

"You seem to know a lot about demons," Parisa said.

"I used to do a little bit of spell casting." Darla said, "Mostly water related spells. So, I have studied various demons. Collectors are one of the ones that I studied. Which makes it all the more ironic that I was captured by one and put into his collection."

"Is there was way to avoid being captured by a collector?" Parisa asked.

"Usually by having a creature protect you," Darla answered, "but it has to be one that the collector cannot use his sleep spell on. There are some creatures that have a natural immunity and some will develop one after having had the spell used on it. Like Ely, now has an immunity from the spell because the collector has used to put him to sleep. That creature can watch over and stop a collector from capturing a person. Most the spell casters have such a creature to protect them from all sorts of demons like collectors."

"So, if the collector finds Nava sleeping, Ely will protect her?" Parisa asked.

"Yes," Darla answered.

"That is good to have that confirmed." Parisa said, "I did not think she would be in too much danger, but Ely had been captured by the collector."

"Nothing is going to harm Nava while Ely is watching her." Darla said, "She fed him and that means he is loyal to her for the rest of her life."

"Even if she goes back through the portal and home?" Parisa asked.

"He cannot get through the portal unless the guardian allows it," Darla answered, "but if she has to go home then Ely will come back to her if she ever comes back through the portal."

"I do not think that the guardian will let Nava take the dragon through." Parisa said, "He did not want to let us through. He tested us because Nava was a little rude to him."

"Then Ely will likely get to go on his way when Nava heads back," Darla said.

"The guardian did say something weird though," Parisa said, "and I am still trying to figure it out."

"What did he say?" Darla asked.

"He said that a human and a fairy were a strange combination." Parisa answered, "We know that Nava is human because she has dwarf blood in her. But I am an orphan and I have no idea who my parents were. The problem is that I do not have wings like fairies or any other features of a fairy, except being smaller than most people my age."

"That is a strange thing," Darla said, "but I cannot help you with that problem. I know more about fairy dust then fairies themselves. Most of what I do know about fairies is information that everyone knows, like the fact that there are some fairies that live in cities like this one and some that make their home in the forest. And that you have to go to the ones that live in the forest if you want fairy dust. Maybe once we figure out how to reverse the spell, the fairies here can give you some answers."

"I hope so," Parisa said.

They left the stable and moved on to the next building.

Narda heard a noise that bought her out of the dream. She was dreaming that she was home and her father was holding her tight, scared that if he let her go that she would disappear on him. She had tried to tell him that she was not going away ever again, but the words would not come out.

The noise came again. It sounded like an animal hissing. Narda sleepily opened her eyes. Ely's head was visible and he was the one hissing at someone coming up the hill. At first Narda could not see who was there, then she saw the outline of a man. Slowly the man came into focus in the light of the torches that were hung outside the door to the castle. Narda recognized the man as the one who took Laken. She blinked a couple times as she could not believe that he was there. Ely was between Narda and the man. The man pointed at Ely and said something that Narda could not quite hear. Nothing happened. The man tried it again, but still nothing happened.

Ely inhaled some air and exhaled a jet of flame. It reached the man and the man had to jump back from it. He still had to put out some of flames on his clothing. Ely hissed again and inhaled to do it again. The man backed away from Ely and Narda.

Narda wanted to stay awake, but her eyelids felt too heavy to stay open. She closed her eyes and was asleep in less than a minute.


"Parisa," Darla called from outside the house that Parisa had just entered to start searching. Parisa turned and went back outside. Darla was looking toward the castle entrance. Parisa looked, but did not see anything.

"What did you see?" Parisa asked.

"Dragon's flame," Darla answered.

"Do you think we should check it out?" Parisa asked,

"We can come back to searching." Darla answered, "The spell will not work on Ely, but who knows what else the collector has to use. And he must be pretty angry that part of his collection is gone."

"Okay," Parisa said.

Parisa and Darla headed back toward the castle.

When they go there, they found Narda asleep wrapped in the blanket and Ely lying beside her. Ely looked up at them briefly before putting his head back down.

"I think they are fine," Parisa said. Parisa and Darla turned and went back to their search.

Narda felt the dew on her cheek and eye lashes. She opened her eyes to see a pink and orange streaked sky above her. The blanket was tucked up to her chin and there was a warm, breathing thing nestled close to her. Narda looked around, but did not see anything out of the ordinary. Parisa and Darla were not back. Narda used the blanket to wipe the dew from her face before she sat up. Ely was the thing pressed up against her. He was still sleeping. Narda carefully got up. She managed to do it without waking Ely. She walked down the hill to the closest house. She found some water there to wash up. When she was finished, Narda went back up to where Ely was and sat down next to him where it was warmest. She pulled the blanket back over herself to keep warm.

Narda looked out over the city. It had some similarities to Proster in the layout of streets, with an area for a market, streets that were mainly shops, and streets that were with just houses for the people to live in. There was less space between the castle and the wall around the city. In Proster, there were whole neighbourhoods between the two, but here there was between four and six cross streets.

Beyond the walls, Narda could see the edge of the field and then the forest. The path that went toward the city sloped down from where it left the forest. The forest might as well have gone on forever, because that was all that could be seen until the mountains in the far distance. There were not that many mountains in Proster that could be seen from the castle.

Narda remembered the one time that she had gone to the tower to try and see the mountains. There had not been much up there besides a window and a door that was locked. She had not been interested in the door; she just wanted to look out the window. That was one of the few times that her father had been angry with her. She had never gone up there again.

She wondered what was happening back at home. Were they worried about where she was? Had they sent out the guards to search the city for her? Her mother would be furious about her not sitting with her at the church service and then disappearing. Her father was more likely to be worried. It would not stop him from dealing with the usual business of running a kingdom. More likely it would cause him to lose some sleep. Narda was sorry about that, but she needed to find Laken and the rest of the children. Her father did not know where to start and she did, so she was in a better position to do something about the man.

Her father would probably have noticed that she had taken the Wizard Slayer by now, so he might be angry over that. But he would be proud of her when she brought back everyone that had been kidnapped. She might not get to go out on any more adventures, but she would do this one right. But she would have to finish this one quickly. Not only would it be better if she got back sooner, but someone might figure out what was happening and come to the rescue. Then they would get the credit and she would be a child being brought back to her parents.

Narda wondered where Parisa and Darla were. She looked over the city again trying to spot them in among the buildings. She could not see them. There did not appear to be any movement in the city at all.

Maybe if they figure out a way to catch the man, they could get him to tell them where he was holding the children. Narda thought about that for a minute. Yes, they were going to have to find him, but she did not think he would tell them anything. Last night they had not been ready for him, but they would have to watchful for the rest of the day. He could show up at any time. Fortunately, Ely had been there to stop the man from getting near her. Narda wondered if Parisa and Darla had run into him on their search and whether they had to defend themselves from him.

The sun appeared over the horizon causing the rest of the darkness in the sky to disappear. It bathed the land with bright yellow light. Behind Narda, Ely moved to try and get his head out of the light. He half succeeded, but could not twist to completely get out of the sunlight. He continued to try and sleep for several more minutes. Finally, he decided that he was going to get anymore sleep and opened his eyes. He blinked at his surroundings for a minute before his eyes adjusted to the brightness.

"Good morning," Narda said.

Ely peered at her as if was not sure about the good part, but that it was definitely morning.

"We should find Parisa and Darla." Narda said as she stood up, "Then we can see what we can find for breakfast."

Ely's ears perked up at the word breakfast and he stuck his nose in the air. He sniffed the air for several minutes before headed down the hill. Narda followed him. They went down the hill and on to a city street. Ely led the way down this street to one of the cross streets where he turned right. At the next street he turned left. He went down this street until he reached a shop and then he stopped. The shop was bakery.

"I say Parisa and Darla before breakfast," Narda said.

Ely gave Narda and look that said he knew that before nodding toward the shop. Narda went to the door and opened it. She did not see Parisa or Darla in the front part of the shop, but she could hear someone moving around.

"Hello?" Narda called. A moment went past before the door to the back room opened and Parisa came out. Darla was not far behind her.

"You are awake," Parisa said.

"I just woke up," Narda said, "and I told Ely if we could find you then we could see what we could find for breakfast, so he found you."

"If you do not mind them to be stale there are some things to eat here," Parisa said.

"Will you eat stale baking?" Narda asked Ely. He nodded.

"Why do not you and Darla go outside and I will bring what I can find?" Parisa said, "Then you do not have to be bent over."

"Okay," Darla said. Narda stepped out of the way and Darla came outside. Narda and Darla sat down on the dirt street. Ely flopped down close enough that he could be handed food.

A few minutes later, Parisa came out carrying a tray piled with baked goods.

"This is some of what looked good enough to eat." Parisa said setting the tray in the middle of the group, "There is more inside if we run out."

"This looks good for now," Narda said. Once Parisa sat down, they each picked out something they wanted to eat. Narda picked out another piece and passed it to Ely.

They ate without talking. Narda, Parisa and Darla ate their fill and Ely kept eating until the tray was empty. When Ely was looking around for more, Parisa took the tray inside the bakery. She came back out again with a full tray. Narda took the tray from Parisa and put it in front of Ely, who proceeded to put his nose in to eat and gobble them as fast as he could.

"Did you find anything?" Narda asked.

"Not yet," Parisa answered, "but we still have a couple streets that we have not searched yet."

"Ely and I searched most of those yesterday." Narda said, "We stopped the next street over."

"We must have missed something," Darla said, "because we have not found any trace of the collector or the children."

"You talked about a spell that we could use to locate the children," Narda said.

"There is a locator spell," Darla said, "but there are several things necessary that we do not have."

"This kingdom has a magician in its employment." Narda said, "He has a room in the castle."

"The items should be in there." Darla said, "We also need a map of the city."

"There is a library in the castle as well," Narda said, "but I did not know if there is a map there."

"We can look and see," Darla said.

"Last night I woke up to see the man coming toward me." Narda said, "He did not get passed because of Ely. I was wondering whether you two had any problems with him."

"We did not see him," Parisa said, "but we did see some flames from where you were so we checked on you. You seemed fine so we went back to searching."

"He must be after you." Darla said, "Otherwise he would have attacked us as well. We would have been in far more trouble if he had. Instead he only went after you."

"Why me?" Narda asked.

"Either you are the next for his collection," Darla said, "or you are what the being controlling him wants. Either way, you should keep Ely close. He will stop the collector from capturing you."

"We all should stay together from now on." Narda said, "Then just in case he is after you, but could not find you. That way we know where each other are at all times."

"Sounds reasonable to me," Darla said.

"Okay with me." Parisa said, "We can skip the searching the buildings then and go straight to the castle."

"Let us go," Narda said as she got to her feet. Parisa and Darla stood up as well. Ely got up as well. They started for the castle.

"We will need to find the collector," Paris said, "and stop him. Otherwise, he will probably keep kidnapping people. And he will continue to pursue us."

"But how do we stop him?" Narda asked.

"Darla, do you know to stop the collector?" Parisa asked.

"I am not sure how to deal with him," Darla answered, "but I do know how hold him somewhere. If you manage to trap him in a circle of fairy dust, then he cannot go anywhere. Once he is inside, then he cannot go anywhere, but it does not do him any damage."

"We will figure out how to deal with him once we have him." Narda said, "Where can we get fairy dust?"

"Hopefully, there will be some in the magician's room," Darla answered, "and then we just need something that we can use as bait."

"We can use me." Narda said, "He came after me last night, so he will likely come after me again."

"Maybe we should deal with the collector before we look for the children." Darla said, "We will be safer once the collector is stuck in one place."

"I am worried about the children," Narda said, "but it is a good idea to deal with the man first."

They reached the castle and went inside. They went to the door to the right and around to the door. They went up the set of stairs that led to the magician's room. At the doorway, Narda and Parisa stopped and let Darla go in by herself. Darla started at the point near the door looking over the contents of the shelves. She slowly worked her way around the room.

Darla was half way around when Narda heard the clinking of claws on the stone stairs. She looked behind her, but did not see anything coming up.

"What is it?" Parisa whispered.

"I am not sure." Narda whispered back, "Stay here." Narda slowly started back down the stairs as quietly as she could. She reached the first turn in the spiral and looked around it. Narda saw Ely coming up the stairs in the smaller form that he had used to help her search the house. Narda went a step down.

"I thought you were going to wait for us outside," Narda said.

Ely looked up at her and shrugged. Narda gave him a long look before turning around and going back up the stairs. She stopped beside Parisa.

"Just Ely," Narda whispered to Parisa. Parisa looked back and saw the small dragon coming up the stairs.

"I did not know he could do that," Parisa whispered.

"I think he can do more than that, but I have not seen him do much more," Narda whispered back. Ely reached the stair below the landing and squeezed his head between Narda and Parisa so that he could see into the room.

Darla was just about finished her examination of the magician's room. She had not touched anything, but a looked at the contents of each jar. Finally, she finished studying the shelves. Darla turned her attention to the magician's table. She looked at it all, but again did not touch anything.

"Can we do either of things we talked about?" Narda asked when Darla had straightened up.

"Yes, we can do both." Darla answered, "We will need to look for a map in the library before we can do the search for the children, but it looks like the ingredients are all here. And there is a large container of fairy dust."

"Then let us go and deal with the man," Narda said.

Ely snorted in agreement. Darla looked down at his head in surprise. She did not say anything about him as she turned around and went to a shelf on the far side of the room. She took down a jar that was just about full of a white powder. She turned back to Narda and Parisa.

"The best place to do this is probably the throne room." Darla said, "The collector may be hesitant to come back to the spot outside and there are more hiding spots in the throne room."

"Okay." Narda said, "Let us go." She turned around and started down the stairs being careful of Ely. Ely followed her down. Parisa and Darla went down after them.

They all went down that set of stairs to the next one and the next one all the way to the door at the landing between the spirals and the dungeon. They went through the door and around the hallway to the door to the throne room.

The throne room had lots of space around, but there were a lot of statues taking up that space. There was a small open area on the left side of the throne room that had not been taken up by statues, but it was not much.

"What do we do about the statues?" Narda asked, "We do not want to hurt any of the people."

"I know a spell that can help us." Darla answered, "We will use the corner that is already open and just create more space over there."

Every one moved to that corner being careful about getting too close to the statues. Once in the corner, Narda, Parisa and Ely moved to stand behind Darla as she faced the rest of the room. Darla opened the lid of the jar and took out a small amount of the powder. She spoke a strange word before blowing the powder off her hand. The statues moved as a group out of the corner without bumping into any other statue. They moved a few feet and then stopped.

"Okay." Darla said, "That should give us all the room we need to work."

"So, I am bait." Narda said, "What do we do?"

"You need to find a spot in this area that is comfortable." Darla said, "Perhaps Ely can go get the blanket that is outside for this. Once you have your spot then I will figure out the straightest route from the door to you and put a circle of fairy dust on the floor. The collector can go over it to get into the circle, but cannot go over it to get out of the circle. Once it is all set up then we will sit and wait for the collector to show up."

Ely came back from outside carrying the blanket with a corner of it in his mouth. He was still small and was having a little bit of trouble with the size of the blanket as it tripping him. He finally reached Narda and set it down.

"Okay," Narda said as she reached down and picked up the blanket. She went to one part and spread the blanket out on the stone floor.

"Maybe I should stay with Narda." Parisa said, "Just in case the collector is watching for me as well."

"Go ahead," Darla said.

Parisa went over to Narda and sat down on the blanket with her. They watched Darla go over to the door and walk several routes from the door to the blanket. Finally she decided on one and poured the fairy dust into a circle on the floor. Ely had gone over to the wall of the throne room and was staying out of the way.

"Okay." Darla said, "I think we are ready." She put the lid back on the jar and went over to the statues. She found a hiding place behind several where she would not be seen by anyone coming in the door of the throne room.

Narda lay down on her side in a way that she could see the door. Parisa lay down on her back. Parisa gave enough room between herself and Narda that a being might think they could take one without waking the other. Ely lay down near the wall and went back to his normal size. There was enough room for him to do so, but he was not able to move very far in any direction.

With everyone in place they waited with no sense in how long it would take or if the collector would show up. Narda and Parisa talked occasionally in whispers, but it was short exchanges and if there were any sounds from anywhere they would stop and not pick up the conversation for half an hour or more. Parisa fell asleep for a while. Ely fell asleep as well, but he did not snore too loudly so they left him alone. The hours inched past.

Narda found herself counting the number of statues in her line of sight. She noticed that there were purple and gold silks hanging from various points on the walls and from the ceiling. They were not very big, but there were about ten of them that Narda could see. The stones in the floor were harder to see and thus harder to count. The wall on the far side of the room was too far away for Narda to want to try and count the stones in it. She slowed her breathing and listened to the sounds around her. She could hear Parisa breathing and Ely's light snores. Occasionally she could hear Darla changing position to get comfortable again. The statues were silent. Once in a while she could hear the wind blow through a draft point in the castle, but could not identify where that point was. There were creaks and groans of the castle itself.

Ely woke up and was suddenly alert. Narda closed her eyes until she was looking through her lashes. Parisa had woken up, but she remained still. Darla did not make a sound, but Narda was sure that she had been alerted as well. Slowly, Ely turned invisible starting from his tail and ending with his snout.

The castle door opened and the man came inside. Narda was sure that he was walking on the floor, but he moved much too smoothly and she could not hear any footsteps. The collector smiled to himself as he crossed the room along the route that Darla predicted he would. The smiled disappeared when he crossed into the circle of fairy dust and could not get out.

When he entered the circle of fairy dust his appearance changed. Before he had been of average height and average size for a middle aged man, his clothes had been brown pants and tunic with brown shoes, and his face was tanned with brown eyes that matched the brown hair that was brushed back like many men slick their hair back. He had been so average that everyone's eyes would have gone over him if they were not purposely looking for him. Now that he was in the circle of fairy dust his appearance changed. His skin was now grey. His eyes were black and his outfit was made up of stitched together brown rags. He had no shoes on, but his finger and toenails were black claws. He did not have any hair and his nose was much smaller. He had no lips, just a mouth that as he screamed with frustration showed black teeth and a pink tongue.

Narda felt the cold fingers of fear go up her spine and she swallowed just to make sure that there was still moisture in her mouth. Darla came out from behind the statues and Parisa sat up. Narda took her eyes away from the collector and slowly sat up.

"Now, he cannot move." Darla said, "So, he cannot harm us."

The collector screamed again in frustration. It was high pitched and echoed off the walls of the throne room making Narda want to put her hands over her ears.

"Are you sure?" Narda asked.

"I am sure." Darla answered, "If he could get out, he would have already."

"So, what do we do with him?" Parisa asked.

"We cannot let him out as he would attack us." Darla answered, "Most physical weapons do not do him any harm. He is immune to most types of magic. He will not answer any of our questions even if we could speak his language. I am not sure what we can do about him. I would have to look up collectors to figure out how to get rid of him."

"Can we just send him home?" Parisa asked.

"Collectors do not have a specific home." Darla answered, "Nor do they come from a different plane of existence. They are created on this plane and they claim spots as their home. He has claimed this kingdom as his home, which is why he has been bringing his collections here."

"I think I know how we can get rid of him," Narda said.

"How?" Darla asked.

"Dragon fire," Narda answered.

"I am not sure if that would work," Darla said

"He did not want to get close to it last night." Narda said, "When Ely threatened him, the collector backed off."

"We can try it," Darla said.

"Ely," Narda called.

Ely became visible in the same way as he had turned invisible, except starting at his snout and ending with his tail. The collector screeched again as Ely inhaled air. Ely exhaled flame. It engulfed the collector and the screeching stopped. The flame also touched a couple of the statues, but as they were stone they were not affected. When the flame was gone there was nothing left of the collector, but a pile of ashes in the circle of fairy dust.

"Dragon fire worked," Narda said looking at the ashes. The fear had let go and she could feel the relief of the collector being gone.

"Can he come back from ashes?" Parisa asked.

"Not that I know." Darla answered, "Most things, once they are a pile of ashes, are dead and do not come back."

"What should we do with the ashes?" Parisa asked.

"Leave him." Narda answered, "We will ask the fairy king what to do with him when we get everyone around here back to normal. Let us go look for the map of the city."

Everyone walked around the circle of fairy dust on the way to the door to the curving hallway. They went back up the sets of stairs, but this time Narda led the way to the library, rather than the magician's room. Ely had gone back to being half his normal size so that he could follow them around. Reaching the library, Darla went inside and the rest of them stayed at the entrance. Darla started to the right of the door and looked over the shelves. She picked up the book on herbs for novice spell casters and looked at it before putting it back. She continued on as she studied the spines of the books on the shelves.

Half way around the room, Darla stopped and pulled a book off the shelf. It was twice the height of most of the rest of the books and the binding was a dusty red. The front called it an atlas.

"This should help us," Darla said as she opened it. Dust sprung from the pages of the book and hung in the air causing Darla to sneeze. She carefully turned the pages and looked them over. More dust kept coming off the book and the air moved that was from turning the pages pushed the dust around that was already in the air. Darla was forced to hold the book at arm's length as she went through it.

"Is it normal for a book to have that much dust on it?" Parisa asked as she held her sleeve of her mouth and nose to protect them from the dust that was in the air.

"It depends on the book and how long it has sat in one place without being dusted," Narda answered as she too put her sleeve in front of her mouth and nose.

"This room must not have been used in a couple hundred years then," Parisa said.

"It is not the," Darla started before being interrupted by a sneeze, "normal amount of dust." Darla sneezed again. "It is a-choo. A protection spell."

"It works well then," Parisa said.

"Can we use the book then?" Narda asked.

Darla tried to answer several times, but sneezing kept interrupting her. Finally she nodded. She closed the book and the dust stopped pouring off the pages. She was still sneezing as she headed for the door. Narda and Parisa turned and started down the stairs. Ely was already on his way down as he had started when the book had been opened. Darla followed Narda and Parisa. They went down the set of stairs and went up the sets of stairs that would take them to the magician's room.

In the magician's room, Darla set the book on the table before going to the shelves. She found what she was looking for and took the jar down from the shelf. The jar appeared to be full of pebbles. Darla opened the jar and sprinkled a few pebbles on top of the book while reciting a word.

Narda and Parisa watched all this from the doorway. Darla put the lid back on the jar and put it back on the shelf. Then she went back to the book and opened it. This time the dust did not pour off the pages. Darla flipped through the book until she found a map of the city. She carefully set the book flat on the table and made sure that it would stay open to that page. Darla took several jars down from the shelves and poured a little of the contents of each into a bowl. When she was finished that, she mixed it all together.

"Narda, I need you to think of a person who is in the collection." Darla said, "Picture that person in your mind."

Narda pictured Laken in her mind. Darla took Narda's hand and ran it down the open page of the atlas. Then she poured the contents of the bowl over the page of the book while reciting some words. A black powder poured out of the bowl and spread out on the page. It sat dormant for a minute before slowly moving. It all gathered in one spot on the page and Darla stopped reciting the words. She put the bowl down and leaned over the page.

Narda and Parisa stepped into the room to see the page as well. All the black powder was gathered on top of a long building that looked to be tavern in a section of the city that was behind the castle.

"We searched that building," Parisa said, "last night. We did not see any trace of the children or the collector."

"Let us go through the building again." Narda said, "The collector managed to steal the children without leaving a trace, perhaps he did the same when he left them in the building. That would make it harder to find them."

"It would be a good idea." Darla said, "This spell is not perfect, but it is right most of the time. We may have missed something."

"We better hurry then," Parisa said pointing to the window. The purplish pink of sunset could be seen through the window.

Narda, Parisa, and Darla headed down the stairs followed by Ely.

They left the castle and went around it to the right section of the city. They went down the hill to the street. Darla took the lead as they went through the streets to the building. The building was twice the length of the buildings around it. There were windows along the whole side so the inside was visible. The group went through the door. There were three statues inside among the tables and chairs. One was behind the bar with a cloth and mug in hand. The other was sitting on a chair was his head on the table and his hand wrapped around the handle of a mug. The third was a woman carrying a tray of mugs toward a door beside the bar.

Ely started to sniff around as Narda, Parisa and Darla started searching in dim light of the sunset. The orange light seemed to create more shadows then dispel them. Ely headed in the door beside the bar. Narda followed him. This room contained barrels, bottles and a small kitchen area. There was a man standing there stirring a pan of something over a fire that had died out. Ely went to the corner where the barrels were stacked. He sniffed around a barrel that was beside a stack. It did not look completely out of place with where it was, but it was the only barrel that was not stacked at least two high. Ely stopped, looked at Narda and snorted that he had found what they were looking for.

"Parisa, Darla," Narda called, "in here." Narda went over to the barrel and tried to move it, but it would not budge. Parisa and Darla came through the door and saw what Narda was doing. They came over to help her. The three of them working got the barrel to move. They pushed it to be in front of the rest of the barrels. Once it was out of the way, Narda went down on her knees and searched the area with her fingers. She dusted away some of the dirt and found a handle. She pulled on it with all her might. There was a snapping sound and then the trap door slowly lifted. Narda pulled it all the way open. The top of the trap door came to rest on the nearby barrels. Narda scrambled down the wooden staircase that went down to the cellar. The cellar was the length and width of the building above it. It was packed dirt. There were several crates sitting on the dirt floor. None of them were stacked. There were two torches providing light, one on each wall. Sitting on the crates and on the floor were ten children. Laken was one of them, as well as Oriel. There was a girl, Narda recognized as the daughter of the blacksmith, holding a baby. The rest were from the ages of two to eight and they looked scared.

"Narda," Laken said standing up, "what are you doing here?"

"Parisa and I saw the collector take you and we followed him here." Narda answered, "Come on, we need to get out of here."

"He is going to come back here," the daughter of the blacksmith said.

"We dealt with the collector." Narda said, "Come on."

All of the children got up and went up the stairs. Narda made sure that they were all up before following them. Parisa and Darla had gathered the children all together at the top of the stairs and were ready to leave the tavern when Narda came out of the cellar. Narda pushed the door to close it before leading the way out of the back room. The children were all silent and still looked scared. They did not make much noise and stayed together as a group. Narda and Parisa led the way with Laken right behind them and Darla leading the children. Ely was behind them to make sure that no one strayed.

They left the tavern and started back toward the castle. The sun had gone down now, but the moon was full and provided plenty of light for the group to see their way. They were half up the street when shapes came out of the darkness toward them. Even with the light it took a few moments for Narda to recognize the shapes as frost wolves. Narda looked back down the street and saw another group of frost wolves behind them.

The frost wolves were twice the size of any other wolf Narda had ever seen. Their fur was a mixture of grey, blue and black with glowing blue eyes. There was ice hanging off their fur and when they breathed out their breath was visible even though the night was warm.

"Darla, get them inside," Narda yelled as she pulled out the Wizard Slayer. Parisa pulled out her sword as well. Narda handed the Wizard Slayer to Laken and took out her bow. She fitted an arrow into it. Laken had no trouble lifting the sword as he was five feet and had been trained to handle a sword. The three got ready for the attack as Darla ushered the children into the closest two storey building. Ely made sure that all the children were inside before changing to his full size. Laken looked in astonishment at Ely for a moment before turning his attention back to the approaching frost wolves.

The frost wolves were snarling as they came. There were five coming from either direction. Narda did not see anymore, but she sensed that they were being watched. Once the first frost wolf was within shooting distance, Narda let loose her first arrow. The frost wolf dodged the arrow and it hit the street without harming anything. Narda notched another arrow. She shot it as the first frost wolf was close enough to attack Parisa. Parisa thrust her sword at it. Narda's arrow headed toward the next frost wolf. The wolf tried to dodge the arrow, but was not fast enough and the arrow entered the frost wolf's side. The frost wolf howled in pain before charging at Narda.

Parisa managed to fend off the frost wolf's attacks. She stabbed it several times causing it to bleed black blood, but that did not slow it down much. Ely was busy with the frost wolves that had been coming at them from the other direction. He had charged into the group and was using his claws to attack them. The frost wolves were concentrating on Ely and not paying any attention to the rest of the fight.

Laken slashed the frost wolf that had launched itself at Narda as it went passed him. He managed to cut open the frost wolf's side causing it to collapse just short of Narda. The frost wolf tried to get up, but it could not move that much. Narda took out her hunting knife and finished the frost wolf before going back to her bow and notching another arrow. Laken was fighting the frost wolf that had reached him.

There were two more frost wolves coming toward them. Narda shot an arrow at the closest one. She hit this one in the neck and the frost wolf howled in pain before collapsing. The next frost wolf changed its course from heading toward Parisa, who was still fighting the first wolf, to heading for Narda. Narda fitted another arrow and shot it at the frost wolf. The frost wolf dodged before launching itself at Narda.

Laken had done some damage to the frost wolf that he was fighting, but it was strong enough that Laken was having trouble taking it down. Parisa was still stabbing at the frost wolf that she was fighting and it was beginning to weaken the frost wolf. Narda put another arrow in her bow and shot it at the frost wolf that had launched itself at her. The arrow missed. Narda did not have enough time to notch another arrow before the frost wolf reached her, so she rolled forward causing the wolf to land where she had been standing. Narda finished her roll and spun back to face the frost wolf. The frost wolf snarled at her as Narda pulled out her hunting knife again. The frost wolf started to move in a circle and Narda moved with it. Narda watched the frost wolf for any sign of what it was going to do, so that she could figure out how to counter it.

The frost wolf suddenly charged her. Narda dodged just before it reached her and she stabbed the frost wolf with her hunting knife. Then she moved farther away from the frost wolf as it made a fast turn to bite her. The frost wolf's jaw met air, but it was close. They went back to circling.

Parisa's frost wolf collapsed finally from all the stab wounds. Parisa finished the frost wolf off. Parisa looked around and saw the situation Narda was in. She ran to help Narda. Parisa went after the frost wolf with her short sword in hand. The frost wolf seemed to be fixed on Narda until Parisa got close enough then it turned and clamped its jaw over Parisa's leg. As Parisa screamed in pain, Narda crossed the area to the frost wolf and stabbed the frost wolf. The frost wolf let go of Parisa's leg, but did not have time to turn to Narda before she stabbed him again. This time she stabbed it in the neck. The frost wolf collapsed, but Narda continued to stab it. She stabbed it until she was absolutely positive that it was dead. Narda moved around the frost wolf's body to Parisa. Parisa was sitting on the street. The frost wolf had ripped her pants and ripped the skin underneath, but it did not look too bad.

"Are you okay?" Narda asked Parisa.

"I will be fine once this is over and it can be dealt with properly," Parisa answered.

Both Narda and Parisa looked over at Laken, who was still fighting with his frost wolf. The frost wolf had done some damage to Laken and Laken had done some damage to the frost wolf. Laken was getting tired and the frost wolf looked to be just warming up. Narda put her hunting knife away and picked up Parisa's short sword. She straightened up and ran toward the frost wolf. Both combatants were too busy with each other to notice her. Narda reached the frost wolf and plunged the short sword into the frost wolf's back. The frost wolf howled and started to turn toward Narda. This gave Laken the opportunity to cut the frost wolf's throat. The frost wolf collapsed.

Laken bent over to try and catch his breath. Narda looked over at Ely. He was still fighting two more frost wolves, but between his dragon fire and his claws it did not look like the frost wolves would survive long.

Something caught Narda eyes. She turned toward it. Something was moving along the roof top of the buildings. Narda took out her bow and notched an arrow. She let the arrow fly. The arrow hit whatever it was and caused it to fall off the roof. It landed on the street below. Narda walked over to it. Lying on the street was a hellcat with an arrow stuck in its neck.

"What is a hellcat doing here?" Parisa asked from behind Narda. Narda glanced back and saw that both Parisa and Laken had followed her.

"I think I know who the collector was working for," Narda said. The answer dawned on Parisa, but Laken just looked confused.

"Collectors usually work for a being more powerful than themselves." Narda explained, "The collector was using this town for his collections. We killed the collector and now the being that it was working for wants revenge. When Parisa and I followed the collector through the portal, the guardian of the portal made us face off against some hellcats to prove that we had what it took to enter the portal. If there are hellcats here then the portal guardian is the one who the collector is working for."

"So, what do we do?" Laken asked, "We can not go up against the portal guardian ourselves and we can not just go up to him with the request to go back through the portal. And who knows what else he is going to send to kill us."

"We need to get everyone back to the castle." Narda said, "The answer to the curse must be there. If we can break the curse, we can get help getting home."

"Let us get moving," Parisa said, "before anything else shows up."

Narda, Parisa and Laken went to the house where Darla had taken the children. Narda went into the house while Parisa and Laken stood guard. Narda went up the stairs and found them all in a bedroom.

"We need to get to the castle before anything else attacks," Narda told Darla.

"Okay," Darla said. The two of them herded the children down the stairs and out of the house. Ely was now waiting with Parisa and Laken.

Narda and Parisa took the lead with Darla taking care of the children. Ely and Laken followed them. Ely made sure that none of the children were left behind and Laken watched for anything that might attack them.

They went through the streets heading back to the castle. A couple times Narda thought she saw creatures on the roof of buildings as they went passed, but when she turned to look the creature was gone. Nothing came out and attacked them. They got to the base of the hill and started to climb. Below them there seemed to be eyes peering at them from the darkness, but nothing followed them up.

The group went around the castle to the entrance. They went inside and closed the doors behind them. There was nothing inside the throne room waiting for them. Darla took the children over to where the blanket was, while keeping them away from the ring of fairy dust. Narda, Parisa and Laken found the bar for the door and put it in place. Once they had done that they went to where the Darla and the children were. They sat down.

Narda went through the stuff she and Parisa brought and took out what little they had for bandages. She gave some to Laken for him to bandage his wounds then she took the rest and used it to bandage Parisa's leg.

"What are we going to do?" Parisa asked as she watched Narda, "We can not go home, there is no food in the castle, and if we leave we risk battling whatever he sends after us. We do not know enough about magic to figure out how to lift spell that is on this city."

"Nothing is attacking us here." Narda said, "Either he believes that we are trapped and intends to hurt us that way, or his creatures can not enter here. If he is intent on hurting us, why not take us out right away by having something waiting for us?"

"All the statues are fairies." Darla said, "It is most likely that there is something in the castle that protects it."

"It did not protect the people from the spell that made them all into statues," Laken said.

"There are no spells that most can cast that would be powerful enough to turn a whole city into statues." Darla said, "This is a curse, not just a magic spell. Curses can be more powerful no matter who casts it. The protection might be useful for magic spells and not for curses. It is not uncommon, because very few beings use curses. The being that did this curse might still be trying to recover from it."

"We believe that the being that cursed this place is the portal guardian," Narda said.

"Why would a portal guardian curse this place?" Darla asked, "It can not leave the portal it guards, so it can not use the city itself. And a portal guardian using a collector makes even less sense."

"We are not sure the whys of it all," Narda said, "but we are just talking what we know and trying to figure it all out from there. Right now, we need to figure out who could lift the curse."

"Lifting cursing can be very difficult." Darla said, "My knowledge of curses is very limited.

"Perhaps the books in the library can help us." Parisa said, "The answer could be in there."

"Could be," Darla said.

"Let us sleep for tonight." Narda said, "We are all tired. Tomorrow, we will search the library for an answer."

Everyone was quiet for a while, but no one seemed ready for sleep. Narda went through the bag again and took out the last of the dried meat. She broke it into enough pieces for everyone to have some and then passed it around. Each of them took a piece and ate it. The blanket was not big enough for everyone, so Narda went up to the one room with bunks and took the rest of the blankets from the room. She brought them back. Darla helped her spread them out. Everyone got some space on a blanket, except Ely who lay down by the doors. Everyone else lay down.

Narda heard some of them fall asleep, but she knew that not all of them had. She did not want to get up and disturb anyone, but she found herself unable to sleep. Narda lay there for a long time staring up at the ceiling hoping for sleep to come.

## NARDA HAS TO FIGURE OUT HOW TO LIFT THE CURSE AND GET THE CITY BACK TO NORMAL

Narda woke to the sound of Ely moving around. She sat up and looked around. Everyone else was still asleep, even those that had not looked like they were going to go to sleep at all. Ely was pacing in front of the door. Narda quietly stood up and went over to Ely. Ely stopped pacing and looked at Narda. Narda lifted the bar off the door. She opened the door and looked out. There were no creatures within sight. Narda opened the door the rest of the way and let Ely go out. She did not close the door, but sat down in front of the doorway instead. It was still dark out, but there was a faint light over the horizon. Narda sat there looking over the view as the light got brighter.

Narda felt a longing for home as she looked out at the streaks of orange and pink stretching out from the horizon to the rest of the sky. At home, she had her comfortable bed, a kitchen where she could go find food any time, and her father, who could have figured out the answer to the curse without difficulty. He knew about this magic stuff and would have the answer to the problem facing her. Her father would have dealt with it long before now and would have had the children back home before night fell. But Narda was not that good. This was just her first adventure on her own and she was stumped by a curse. If she could figure out how to lift the curse she could get help from the king. From there she would get the children home and everything would go back to normal. Back home, she would get more respect from her mother for getting through all this and she would be back in her own bed. Her own bed sounded nice.

Someone moved. Narda looked over and saw Parisa was the one who moved. Parisa got up and came over to where Narda was sitting. Parisa sat down beside Narda.

"Watching the sun rise?" Parisa asked.

"Yes," Narda turned back to looking out the door. The sun was peeking over the horizon and the sky was full of orange and pink.

"What is wrong?" Parisa asked.

"I miss my bed." Narda answered, "The feel of the sheets when I first get into it, the warmth of the quilt and the softness of the pillow. The memory is nothing like the actual feel of the warmth and comfort of my bed. I did not need the bed curtains or even the rest of the room, just the bed would be wonderful."

"The king must have a room up there." Parisa said, "Why not stay in his bed? It is probably very comfortable."

"Because it is his bed." Narda answered, "It is not the same and it feels like trespassing."

"We have been wandering this whole kingdom, going into places that these people would not allow us." Parisa said, "We have been eating their food and feeding it to Ely."

"That is different." Narda said, "We have not been

sleeping in their beds or going through their dresser drawers."

"True," Parisa said, "but we do the rest because we have to. We do not have to sleep in their bed or go through their dresser drawers. But if you would be more comfortable."

"That is not the point." Narda said, "The point is that I want to go home. I want to lift this curse so that we find some way to go home."

"I have been thinking about that actually," Parisa said, her eyes suddenly on her twisting fingers.

"What?" Narda asked.

"If it turns out that I am a fairy." Parisa said, "I think I will stay here. This is a place for fairies and so I think I would feel more at home here."

"That makes sense," Narda said, "especially since you do not have much of a home back in Proster. You will be happier here."

"I'm glad you are not upset over me staying here," Parisa said.

"I am going to miss you," Narda said, "but I am not going to hold you back from something like this."

"Thank you." Parisa said giving Narda a hug, "You are a true friend."

Narda hugged Parisa back. When they let go they smiled at each other before turning back to the sun rise.

The sun had come up and Ely had come back, by the time everyone else woke up. Narda, Laken and Ely went down the hill into the city and found food for the group. They brought it back so that everyone could have breakfast.

Once breakfast was finished Narda and Darla left Parisa and Laken watching the children while they went up the stairs to the library. This time both of them scanned the shelves. They looked at the titles of all of the books without any luck. None of the books were on curses and very few of them were on magic.

Narda took down the book on herbs for novice spell casters. She flipped through it. No dust came off, so it was not protected. The book fell open to a page marked with a piece of scarlet fabric. Narda read the page.

"Darla." Narda said, "This book is marked on a page about how to avoid being under a curse." Darla came over to where Narda was standing and looked at the page.

"The portal guardian would not need that because he would not be in the area of the curse." Darla said, "Someone must have known that the curse was coming, or it was not the portal guardian who put the curse on this city."

"What was the spell book on the magician's table?" Narda asked.

"I do not remember looking at it," Darla answered.

"Let us go look at it now," Narda said closing the book. They left the library and headed up to the magician's work room. The spell book was still sitting open on the table. The page it was open to a spell on dealing with magic created rashes. Narda closed the book and looked at the cover. The title was Curses and Other High Jinx.

"The court magician put a curse on the city?" Darla said, "It must have drained him almost completely to do it."

"How does he fit in with the portal guardian?" Narda said as she flipped through the spell book. About the middle of the book, she came on a curse that turned people to stone.

"Here it is," Narda said.

"Does it say how to lift the curse?" Darla asked.

"Just a minute," Narda said as she skimmed the page. She skimmed the rest of the page and then flipped to the next one and continued to skim. When she finished, Narda looked up at Darla.

"I think we have to kill the person who put the curse on the city to lift it," Narda said handing the spell book to Darla. Darla took the book and went through the spell herself.

"No, we do not have to kill the person." Darla said, "The person who cast the curse can lift it without us having to kill them. It is if they are not willing to lift the curse that we would have to kill them."

"So, we need to find the court magician and get him to lift the curse." Narda said, "Where do we start looking? If he took the herb mixture he should not be a statue, but if he did not take the herb mixture he could be a statue down in the throne room."

"Let us try this," Darla set the book down on the work table and went over to where the atlas was still sitting on the table. She picked up the atlas and poured the powder back into the bowl. Darla picked up a quill and ran it over the page. Then she put the atlas back and repeated the pouring of the powder with the reciting of words that she had done before to find the children. The powder poured on to the page from the bowl. This time the powder stayed where it was.

"It did not work," Narda said.

"That suggests that the court magician is not in the city," Darla said.

"If he was a statue, would the spell tell you where he

is?" Narda asked.

"No." Darla answered, "The spell does not search for people who have become objects."

"I will go down to the throne room and see if anyone of the statues down there looks like a court magician," Narda said.

"I will try the spell on other maps." Darla said, "Perhaps he had enough energy to leave the city." Darla poured the powder back into the bowl.

Narda turned and went down the sets of stairs.

In the throne room, Parisa and Laken were keeping the children entertained and from being scared, while keeping them on the blankets. Parisa looked to Narda, but Narda went to the statues and looked them over. Laken got up and went over to Narda.

"What did you find?" Laken asked.

"We need to be looking for the court magician." Narda answered, "He can break the spell and then we will get help getting everyone home."

"How long with this take?" Laken asked, "I can not wait to get back."

"I do not know how long exactly," Narda answered, "but soon I hope."

Laken went back to the blankets and Narda kept looking over the statues.

They were lots of statues in the throne room. Most of them looked to have money to spend on clothes. There was a few near the back of the group that had clothing that was not quite the same quality. None of them were clothed in something that a court magician would wear. When she had checked all of the statues, Narda went back up the stairs to the magician's work room.

Narda found Darla standing at the table looking at the atlas.

"Did you find anything?" Narda asked as she entered the room.

"I think the magician is hiding out in the forest," Darla answered. Narda got close enough that she could see that the powder was gathered in one area that the map indicted was forest, not far from what appeared to be the wall of the city.

"That should not be too hard to find," Narda said.

"Depending on how thick the forest is it might be harder than you think." Darla said as she picked up the quill, "Not to mention anything that the portal guardian sends after you." Darla dipped the quill in the container of ink she opened and drew a circle around where the powder was. Then Darla shook the powder back into the bowl.

"Parisa, Laken and I will go get the magician." Narda said, "You stay and watch the children. Ely can come with me. As long as you stay in the castle you should be fine."

"You need to be careful," Darla said, "with the collector's behaviour, it is possible that you are the portal guardian's target."

"I might have been next for the collector's collection too." Narda said, "We need to find the magician so that we can get those children home."

"Just be careful," Darla said.

"I will be," Narda said as she picked up the atlas. She folded the corner of the age over as a book mark and then closed the book before heading down the stairs. Darla followed Narda down.

In the throne room, Narda and Darla found Parisa

and Laken still keeping the children entertained. Narda and Darla went over to the group.

"Are we going home soon?" the blacksmith's daughter asked when they reached the group.

"I hope so." Narda answered, "Parisa, Laken and I are taking Ely and going to look for the court magician in hopes that he can help us. You all will stay with Darla. We will be back as soon as possible and hopefully we will have a way home at the same time."

"I hope so," the blacksmith's daughter said. Darla sat down on the blanket as Parisa and Laken stood up. They followed Narda away from the blanket. Ely joined them at the door. Once outside the castle, they closed the doors and looked down the hill. There did not seem to be any more creatures waiting to attack them.

Narda took a deep breath.

"Let us go," Narda said. She led the way down the hill. At the bottom, nothing came out and attacked them. The group headed down the street, being watchful of any movement.

They reached the gates to the city without incident. However, right outside the gate, guarding it against anyone leaving were five lizard men. They looked like lizards, but they were about five feet tall with red scales. They had spikes running from the top of their head to the end of their tails. The lizard men's arms and legs were short compared to their thin bodies. Their mouths were open and showed two rows of teeth. All five of them held a long sword in both hands and blue belts around their waists with sheaths attached. And they were all looking at Narda and the group with interest.

"I knew this would not be this easy," Parisa

commented as she pulled out the short sword. Laken took out the Wizard Slayer. Narda took out her bow and notched an arrow in it, but she was not sure how well it would work against the scales of the lizard men.

Ely charged forward with his claws extended and exhaling a burst of flame. The lizard men jumped out of the way of the flame and were fast enough to dodge the swipe of Ely's claws. One jumped back as it swung its sword. Narda flinched as the sword came down in Ely. The sword hit Ely's scales and bounced off without harming Ely, but the sword vibrated on impact causing the lizard man's arms to vibrate as well. Before the lizard man could do anything, Ely whirled around and smacked it with his tail.

Narda noticed the rest of the lizard men coming toward Parisa, Laken and her. She shot at the one closest to her. The arrow bounced harmlessly off the lizard man's scales. She notched another arrow and shot it. This arrow hit the lizard man in the eye. The lizard man stopped and broke off the shaft of the arrow before continuing toward Narda.

Laken was already in combat with a lizard man. The lizard man was faster than Laken, but the Wizard Slayer did damage every time Laken managed to hit the Lizard man.

Parisa was struggling at dodging the lizard man that was attacking her. She could not seem to get the short sword close enough to hit the lizard man and it would not have done much good if she could touch him with it. But she kept dodging and looking for a weak spot.

Ely had grabbed the fourth that had headed their direction. The lizard man had already lost his sword and was fighting claw to claw with Ely. Ely was bigger than the lizard man. The lizard man was faster, but that did not seem to be helping it.

Narda put her bow away and took out her hunting knife. It would not do much good against the lizard man unless she found a weak spot, but it was the only weapon she had left. The lizard man came at her swinging its sword. Narda rolled to avoid that swing. She ducked in close, while the lizard man was recovering, to jab her hunting knife at the lizard man's belly, but the hunting knife did not do any damage. The lizard man lifted its sword and swung again. Narda jumped back before the sword could hit her. She moved to her left as the lizard man recovered. The lizard man held its sword up and moved while watching Narda. Narda started to close the space between them and the lizard man brought down the sword. She moved to the right enough that the sword missed her and continued forward to the lizard man. She jabbed her hunting knife up into the lizard man's chin. The lizard man made a gurgling sound and green blood bubbled out of the wound. Narda jerked her hunting knife out and jumped back out of the way. The lizard man collapsed on top of his sword.

There was a hissing sound and Narda looked down at her hunting knife. The green blood was eating at the metal. She wiped it off on the lizard man's blue belt. Then she looked around. Ely had fried one of the lizard men, but the first one that he had knocked out was back. It had already lost its sword and was raking its claws across Ely's scales without doing any damage to Ely.

Laken was an equal swordsman to the lizard man, but the lizard man was winning because he was fighting dirty. They would have their swords locked and he would reach out and scratch Laken. Laken would fight harder to unlock the swords. The Wizard Slayer had taken chunks out of the lizard man, but it was not enough to slow it down.

Parisa was still busy dodging the lizard man's swings with the one she was fighting. Neither side had taken a hit, so far. Narda left Parisa to continue her fight and ran to help Laken. When she reached the fight, Narda slashed at the lizard man's legs. Her hunting knife just bounced off, but it was making it harder for the lizard man to keep its balance. The lizard man continued to fight Laken, but when it could it would try and scratch Narda. At one of the moments when Laken and the lizard man had their swords locked, the lizard man reached out to scratch Narda. Narda jumped out of the way. Before the lizard man was ready Laken yanked the Wizard Slayer free and swung it at the lizard man. The lizard man did not have time to react and the Wizard Slayer went through the lizard man's chest cutting it in half. The two halves fell to the ground and twitched a couple times before becoming still.

"The blood is acid," Narda said as Laken stared down at the corpse while trying to get is breath back. Laken looked to the Wizard Slayer and saw that Narda was right. He wiped the Wizard Slayer off on the lizard man's belt.

Narda looked around. Ely had fried his second lizard man and was working on the one that Parisa had been fighting. Parisa stood and watched Ely bat the lizard man around like it was a toy. Finally, Ely inhaled air and exhaled a shot of flame. The lizard man became charred remains that collapsed to the ground.

"Is everyone all right?" Narda asked.

"I am fine," Parisa answered. Ely snorted that he was fine.

"I am okay," Laken said. His voice sounded shaky so Narda turned back to him. His face was draining of colour and his hands were trembling.

"I think their claws are poisonous," Parisa said looking at Laken.

"I am okay," Laken said as he tried to put the Wizard Slayer back in the straps he had put together to hold it to his back. His hands were shaking too much for him to successfully put the sword away.

"Laken, sit down and rest." Narda said, "If you are not moving the poison will not spread as fast. Parisa, is there anything we can do to treat the poison?"

Laken fell down more than sat down, the Wizard Slayer dropping into the dirt beside him.

"I think there are some plants in the forest that have leaves that will help," Parisa said. Narda looked at the forest it was several yards from them to the trees.

Ely snorted as he leaned down next to Parisa.

"I think he wants you to ride him," Narda said.

"But-" Parisa started.

"Hurry, it does not look like we have much time," Narda shouted to her. Parisa glanced once more at Laken, who went from a sitting position to lying in the dirt with no will of his own. Then she hurried up on Ely's back. Ely flapped his wings and rose in the air. He headed for the forest as fast as he could go with Parisa on his back. Narda went over to Laken. He was still alive. She took his hand in her own.

"Stay with me." Narda said, "Parisa will be back with the leaves as fast as she can."

Narda saw Ely land by the trees. Parisa slid off and disappeared into the trees. Narda continued to watch the spot where Parisa went while talking to Laken.

It felt like a long time before Parisa reappeared and climbed back up on Ely. Ely lifted off and flew back towards Narda and Laken.

"Here they come." Narda told Laken, "Do not leave yet. You can not go home if you die here."

Ely landed near Narda and Parisa slid off his back. She had a handful of leaves. Parisa kneeled beside Laken and opened his mouth. She put several leaves into his mouth and then poured some water in before closing his mouth. Laken swallowed the water and chewed on the leaves. He swallowed again. He gagged a little bit, but Parisa was quickly shoving more leaves into his mouth. She did not let up until he had chewed and swallowed all the leaves that she had brought back.

"That should be enough." Parisa said, "We just need to wait for them to take effect."

Narda squeezed Laken's hand once more before she and Parisa moved back. Laken appeared to fall asleep. As he slept his colour returned and he was doing better.

"How long is he going to sleep?" Narda asked as she checked on the sun's position in the sky.

"I am not sure," Parisa answered.

"Ely, do you think you can carry him?" Narda asked, "You do not have to fly or anything like that. Just carry him, so that he stays with us."

Ely thought about it for a minute before shrugging and nodding. Narda went over and put the Wizard Slayer back in the sheath with her. Then she and Parisa lifted Laken and slung him across Ely's back. They tied him in place so that he would not fall off. Then they started across the field to the right of the gate.

Narda and Parisa walked the yards to the forest together while Ely followed them. Reaching the trees they found a hunting path that went through the trees. Narda went first, Parisa went in second and Ely followed them in. The path was just big enough for one person to walk comfortably. Two people across would have been crowded. Ely stayed near the ground and tried to make himself as thin as possible with Laken on his back.

The forest was made up of deciduous trees, small leafy bushes, moss, moisture, and fog. It was impossible to see anything more than five feet in any direction. Water dripped from the leaves that hung over head as if the clear sky that had been above them when they were in the field had been replaced with storm clouds. The smell of damp earth filled the air as if trying to oppress them and send them away. The dripping of water and the rustling of the leaves could be heard, but there were no sounds in the bushes that suggested animal activity.

"It does not feel like the forest wants us here," Parisa whispered. Narda glanced back at her friend and found her gaze drawn to the path behind Ely. Where there had been one just moments before now stood trees.

"I am not sure that we can back out now," Narda found herself whispering. Parisa glanced back as well.

"So, we continue?" Parisa asked.

"We do not have much choice now," Narda answered. She turned back around and continued along the path.

They walked without talking. Narda searched the fog on either side of the path for signs of anything, but they could have walked passed a whole city and not have seen it. There were no sounds to indict that there was anything out there. Nothing had jumped out to attack them.

"What do we do about finding the court magician?" Parisa's whisper broke into Narda concentration, "You had the map of where he was. Are we going anywhere near the right direction to reach him?"

"I can not tell," Narda answered, "but I do not think we have much choice but going wherever the forest wants us to go. The trees are too close together for us to get far from the path and that is without worrying about the bushes and the moss. Then there is the fog, which is thicker off the path than on it. I am hoping that the forest is willing to take us to the court magician."

"I guess we will find out," Parisa said.

They were quiet as they walked. Narda continued to watch for any signs of any changes in their surroundings. After a while, Narda realized that they could be walking in circles and she would not know the difference. She did notice that she was getting tired and she wanted to find some place to rest.

A moan came from behind Narda. She and Parisa stopped. Laken was waking up. Narda went to Ely and untied Laken. Laken was awake enough to land on his feet.

"Where are we?" Laken asked blinking at their surroundings.

"The forest," Narda answered.

"It looked a lot more inviting from the outside," Laken said.

"We know." Narda said, "We are stuck on this path. I am hoping that it will lead to the court magician. So, far we have not found anything."

"Then we should get moving." Laken said, "The sooner we find the court magician the better." Laken started forward, but he was still recovering from the effects of the poison and was stopped within five steps. He sat down on the path.

"Perhaps we should stop and rest for a few minutes." Narda said, "We are not going to get very far if you can not walk."

Ely lay down on the path. Narda moved near Laken before sitting down. Parisa sat down next to Narda to make a line on the path.

"We could leave the path," Laken suggested.

"We would not get very far," Narda replied.

"Are we headed in the direction that the map says the court magician is?" Laken asked.

"I can not tell anymore," Narda answered, "but I do not think so."

"So, we are lost on a path that could be taking us to a place we really do not want to go," Laken said.

"And the path closed in behind us, so we can not go back," Parisa said.

"I do not think this will end well," Laken said.

"Nothing has attacked us so far." Narda said, "So, whatever is directing us can not want us dead yet. That is a good start. From here we figure out how to survive."

"I am thirteen," Laken said, "you are fourteen, Parisa is eleven. We are not adults. We do not know anything about adventuring. We do not have the skills to survive this. We are three children lost in forest with no way home."

"And no adults around to save us." Narda said, "We

know enough to survive this. No one knows where we are and in the two days that we have been here no one has come through the portal to rescue us. I do not intend to sit around and be killed off by whatever is out there. We have fought hellcats, a collector, frost wolves and lizard men. I am not going to roll over and die now just because we are lost in a forest."

"I am fifteen," Parisa said, "Not eleven."

Narda and Laken looked at Parisa in surprise.

"Really?" Narda said.

"Unlike you I do not get regular meals," Parisa said, "that makes me smaller."

"My father needs to do more for the orphans in the city," Narda said.

Neither Parisa nor Laken had anything to say to that and the conversation did not continue. They sat there listening to the sounds of the forest as they rested.

Narda was just about to suggest that they get up and continue on when she saw a small face appear out of the fog. It was still hard to see and it was peering out from between some bushes. The skin was white with delicate features and emerald eyes filled with wonder. The points of the nose and chin were softened, but the eyes had a little bit of an upward slant. Narda might have brushed it off as her imagination, but it was still there and had not disappeared.

Narda slowly got to her feet as not to scare it. The face stayed where it was. Parisa and Laken assumed without asking that Narda was ready to continue as got to their feet as well. The face did not move. Narda moved forward and the face still stayed where it was. She dashed forward and tried to grab whatever it was that was attached to the face, but it was faster than she was and Narda ended up with a handful of leaves.

"What was it?" Parisa asked.

"I saw a face in this bush," Narda answered, "but it was faster than I am."

"Something is out there," Laken said.

"But it did not attack us," Narda said.

"It will, however, be a little upset that you tried to catch it," Laken said.

"We might as well keep going." Narda said, "It is not likely to come back here."

Narda took the lead again with Parisa behind her and Laken just ahead of Ely. They continued along the path. Despite the amount of time walking and the rest, the light was at the same level and the fog was still the same thickness. And Narda was feeling like she might as well be going around in circles for all the progress she could see. She was getting frustrated and Laken's words were like lead on her mind.

Narda really did not know what was at the end of this path, or even if there was an end to the path. They could be stuck following this path for all of eternity. Or at the end could be certain death. Whatever being was controlling this path could be playing with them before it kills them. The dampness of the forest had already seeped into her clothes making them damp and was beginning to make her feel cold. The longing for her bed at home, came back to Narda with a lot more force than it had this morning. She wanted the warmth and safety of being under her covers. There would be no uncertainty if she could crawl into her own bed.

Narda shook her head slightly. She could not afford to let that thought line go too far. She needed to be here and ready for whatever was ahead. It would be too easy to just give up, but she could not help anyone if she gave up. Laken was wrong. There is an end to this path and the being at the end was not just going to kill them off. If it wanted them dead it had plenty of opportunity already.

The path started to widen by just a bit. If Narda had not been paying attention, she might have missed it.

"I think we are getting close to the end," Narda said.

"Or it could be nothing," Laken's voice was mumbled.

As they went the path got wider. The fog did not lift at all and there were no other signs of anything changing. The path got wide enough that two people could walk beside each other and Parisa moved up to walk with Narda.

The path grew wide enough for three people to walk together and then it suddenly widened out much farther as if they were coming to a clearing. However, there was a wall of fog in front of them. Narda stopped at the wall of fog. So did Parisa.

"This looks like the end," Narda said.

"We need to be prepared for whatever it is that is on the other side of the fog," Laken said holding out his hand.

"But we do not want to appear to be a threat right away." Narda said, "It is never to ones advantage to show all of one's cards at the beginning."

"Fine," Laken said as he dropped his hand.

Narda took a deep breath and walked through the wall of fog. Parisa was a step behind her and Laken and Ely followed.

On the other side of the wall of fog was a clearing. The fog was gone, except for the wall and it was not as damp here. The clearing was large with sun filtering in through the tree branches that swayed in the breeze. The far end of the clearing contained a throne made from an old tree stump. It must have been shaped by magic because it contained none of the marks of a carver. The being that sat on the throne was tall even while seated, would have been willow thin but looked like he ate well, and wore clothing sewn from the leaves that made up the forest around him. He had a gold circlet that wrapped around his head and rested just above his eyes. His face was similar to the one that Narda had seen earlier. The points of his nose and chin were softened with eyes that slanted upward. This man's ears came to points at their tips. His hair was long and silver with matching eyes brows.

The whole group of people the stood in the clearing staring at Narda and her group looked that way. The same facial features and the same thin body structure. Their eyes differed as did the colour of their hair and clothing. There were males, females and children all standing in front of the throne. They all had turned their heads to look at Narda, Parisa, Laken, and Ely.

Narda remembered a story her father had told about forest elves. The story had not been one of his adventures, but a story that had been told to him when he had been young. He believed it to have originated several generations before his father. The story had not painted forest elves in a good light. They were isolationists and rude about it, which explained why the man sitting on the throne was frowning at Narda and her group. Several of the others also looked like they did not like the interruption.

Narda moved toward the throne and the elves moved

aside for her. Parisa, Laken and Ely followed. As Narda got closer to the throne an elf, who was standing just to the left of the throne caught her attention. He did not look to be quite as tall as the elf sitting on the throne, but he was close. His indigo eyes held a different expression from the rest. He had light brown hair was not a long as some of the group and his thin frame had muscles of a fighter. A little voice in Narda's head told her that if she wrapped herself in this elf's arms that she would be safe there and he would make sure that nothing hurt her.

Other thoughts came to her mind as well, but Narda was embarrassed by the direction those were going and quickly squashed them. She did not need any such thoughts filling her head when she was busy with other things. Narda moved her eyes back to the elf sitting on the throne and ignored the cute one with indigo eyes.

Narda stopped a respectful distance from the throne, but she did not bow, neither did Parisa, Laken or Ely.

"Who are you?" the elf on the throne demanded.

"I am Nava," Narda said, "and this is Parisa, Laken and Ely. Who are you?"

"I am King Rian." the elf answered as his eyes narrowed, "This is my forest you have wandered into."

"We did not wander into this forest." Narda said, "We came into this forest intentionally. We came from the fairy city outside the forest."

"What happens in the fairy city is the problem of the fairies who live there," King Rian stated, "It does not matter me and my people. I understand why it might matter to a fairy, but not to a half dwarf, a human and a dragon."

"If I am a fairy, where are my wings?" Parisa

muttered. King Rian ignored Parisa ignored here.

"Why are you here?" King Rian demanded.

"Because we are looking for the court magician from that city." Narda answered, "He is somewhere in this forest. Since what happens in the city does not matter to you then you can just let us get the court magician and we will leave."

King Rian was quiet. He did not look quite as annoyed, but he was not sure about giving in to a stranger's request.

"Kathan," King Rian said.

"Yes, Father," the indigo eyed elf answered.

"Show these people to the spell caster," King Rian said.

"Yes, Father." Kathan said, "This way." Kathan looked at the group. Narda looked at Kathan as he gestured for them to follow him. She followed him with Parisa, Laken and Ely behind her. Kathan went to the trees that were behind the throne and they parted for him. A path opened up as it had been the group had entered the forest and it closed behind them once they were walking along it.

"It is going to take several hours to get to the spell caster." Kathan turned to Narda, "He is in an isolated part of the forest and the path will only take us part of the way there before night fall."

"Okay," Narda said. Kathan turned back around and led the way, while Narda tried to focus on everything other than his perky backside.

The fog had not returned when they entered the forest and neither had the dampness. It was drier and Narda could now see that beyond the trees were just more trees. She could also see bits of the sky through the branches that were overhead. It was early evening according to the angle of the light and the slight change in colour of the sky. Narda could feel the tiredness that came with walking all day and not eating anything since morning, but she was not going to let that slow her down. Especially since they were so close finding the court magician. They would find him and get him to lift the curse. Then this whole adventure would be over.

Narda was so lost in thought that she did not realize that Kathan had stopped until she ran into him. He felt warm and Narda could imagine herself safe in his arms.

"I am sorry," Narda said as she backed away from him.

"We can stop here to rest," Kathan said gesturing to the clearing in front of him.

In the clearing was a tent with open sides set up with four beds, a blanket for Ely, and plates of food ready. Kathan led them to the tent. He sat down on one of the beds. Narda sat down on the one closest to his and Parisa and Laken picked from the other two. Ely lay down on the blanket and immediately put his snout into the plate of meat sitting beside the blanket. Narda picked up the plate that was near the bed she was sitting on. She looked it over. It was a mixture of vegetables and cooked meat. It smelled like the castle kitchen back home just before supper was to be served. Narda's stomach rumbled and she did not waste any more time. She picked up the fork and started to eat. Parisa and Laken did the same. Kathan was much slower at picking up his plate and starting to eat.

By the time Narda was finished eating, Ely was already finished his meat and lying on his back snoring. Parisa had not managed to finish her plateful before falling asleep. Laken was still working on his food. Narda wanted to ask Kathan some questions, but her eye lids kept drifting closed. She finally decided to ask her questions in the morning and curled up on the bed. Her eyes closed on their own volition.

Crickets chirped and night birds were singing their songs when Narda opened her eyes. The moonlight shone in the clearing and provided all the light Narda needed to see around her. Parisa and Laken were asleep. She could not see him, but Narda could hear Ely snore. The only one awake was Kathan, who was sitting cross legged on his bed. He seemed to be mediating.

Narda sat up.

"Are you not tired?" Narda asked Kathan.

"Elves do not require as much sleep as humans or dwarves," Kathan answered, "neither do fairies usually."

"We have had a long several days," Narda said looking at her friends.

"You can rest easy here." Kathan said, "Nothing will hurt you and my father has no further interest in you."

"We appreciate the rest," Narda said.

Kathan did not say anything and the quiet between them stretched.

"Everyone keeps saying that Parisa is a fairy," Narda said, "but she has no memory of being a fairy and she really would like wings if she is a fairy."

"I do not know enough about fairies to know why she does not have wings," Kathan said.

This time Narda did not say anything in response and quiet fell between them again.

"I am sure that the fairies at the city could help her

with those questions," Kathan said.

"That is what we are hoping," Narda said.

The crickets, the birds, and Ely's snoring seemed so far away to Narda even as the quiet again hung between her and Kathan.

"I have been told that elves and dwarves do not get along very well," Narda said, "but no one has ever been able to explain to me why that is."

"That is a long story." Kathan chuckled, "It involves feuds, treachery on both sides, and trading goods. Every single clan of elves has a different version and I am sure that every single clan of dwarves has a different version. For the most part, I believe that it has to do with the different values of elves and dwarves. We value the trees and nature. They value rock and minerals. There are many things that are similar between the races and each one looks solely at the differences."

"What are some of the similarities?" Narda asked.

"Well, to start with both build close knit communities." Kathan answered, "Both use their natural surroundings to provide for themselves. Both trade with other races for things they want that they can not make for themselves. Both have stubborn beliefs about the other. And both take lifemates."

"Lifemates?" Narda asked.

"Elves and dwarves pick one mate for life, rather than have many different mates as humans do," Kathan answered, "Many half elves and half dwarves suffer from that problem. The human side does not really care who they fall in love with as long as it leads to procreation. Elves and dwarves live longer than humans and would rather choose someone who will be there with them from the rest of their life. They are not as worried about procreation. Half-bloods, as they are called, inherit the love for one person, but do not necessarily inherit the longer life."

"My father claimed not to know what love was until the day he set eyes on my mother," Narda said.

"That is a very good example of lifemates," Kathan said, "though with most lifemates the lifemates have very little choice in the matter. Fate, or destiny, which ever you call it interceded on that. This is especially true if the two involved are all elf or all dwarf."

"Has an elf ever fallen for a dwarf?" Narda asked.

"Not in known history," Kathan answered, "but that kind of story would be one that both sides would hide. It is not the kind of thing that anyone would be proud of and if there was child involved that would make things worse."

"I see," Narda said. She slumped back down on the bed.

"That does not mean that it is impossible," Kathan said. Narda glanced at Kathan, but the moon picked that moment to go behind a cloud and she could not see his face. She did not have anything to add to that comment, so she left it hanging and the quiet stretched out between them.

After a while, Narda closed her eyes and let the crickets and birds sing her to sleep.

This time when Narda opened her eyes the sun was up and shining down into the clearing. Kathan was awake and eating the breakfast that was provided, so was Laken and Parisa. Narda sat up and stretched. She saw that Ely was also awake and eating. She picked up the plate from beside her bed and started to eat. This morning the plate was filled with fruit and berries.

The food was gone in minutes. Parisa and Laken were finished about the same time Narda was. Kathan was still eating. Ely had finished already and was sniffing around. He looked like he was ready to go.

Narda was not sure if she wanted to leave. This bed was comfortable, even if it was not her own. And she wanted to stay around Kathan. But King Rian did not want her here. That and she wanted to get Laken and the rest home to their families. She wanted to get home to her family.

Kathan finally finished eating.

"We should be moving along," Kathan said as he stood up.

Narda felt relief as she got to her feet. It was better to be moving than sitting still. Parisa and Laken got up as well and the three followed Kathan away from the beds. He led them on to a path that appeared before him. Ely took the rear as they entered the forest.

The forest was the same as it had been before they had stopped for the night. The sky was blue and the sun was bright above the trees. There were the occasional rustling of animals, but none came on to the path. The birds were singing as they went from tree to tree.

Narda found it peaceful to walk in the forest. The worries seemed distant and there did not feel like there was any hurry to deal with them. Narda embraced the peace, but did not slow her pace.

It was close to noon when the path opened again into a clearing. This time instead of a place to sit and rest the clearing was empty of anything except a man lying on the ground. The man appeared to be asleep. He was dressed in long grey robes with matching slippers. He had brown hair that was long enough to fall in his eyes and a young face. He did not have wings like the rest of the fairies in the city and he was about six feet. And every time he breathed a bubble came out of his mouth. There was a trail of bubbles that were headed up into the sky.

"He is human," Parisa said staring at the man.

"You are looking for the spell caster from the fairy city," Kathan said, "and here he is." Kathan had turned to look at Narda and the group.

"Thank you," Narda said.

"When you are ready to leave a path will open up for you," Kathan said.

"Okay," Narda said. Narda looked up at Kathan and their eyes met. A strange feeling went through Narda, but she brushed it off as she broke eye contact. Kathan went back along the path they had just come from.

"How can the court magician be a human?" Parisa asked.

"I do not know." Narda answered, "We will have to wake him and ask."

Narda went to where the man was lying in the grass. She knelt down and shook his shoulder. He did not stir. She shook his shoulder harder. The man rolled over on to his side and did not wake up. Narda straightened up and kicked the man. The man was rolled over on to his back by the force of the kick.

The man opened his eyes and looked around without moving much.

"Who are you?" the man asked.

"I am Nava," Narda answered, "and this is Parisa, Laken and Ely. We just came from the fairy city, where everyone has been turned to statues by the curse you put on them."

"Can you just let me sleep?" the man asked, "I am tired."

"You can sleep after you lift the curse from the city," Narda answered.

"I can not do that," the man closed his eyes.

"Yes, you can," Narda said, "and you will."

The man did not respond, but his breathing had not quite evened out. Narda kicked him again, sending him a short distance. The man opened his eyes again and looked at Narda.

"That hurt," the man said.

"Why is a human the court magician of a fairy city?" Narda demanded.

"The king liked my qualifications," the man answered, "and I had nowhere else to go."

"How did you as a human get through the portal?" Narda asked.

"I was out looking for herbs when I came across the portal." the man answered, "My mother had told me all about magic and I knew what it was. I went into it. The portal guardian let me through. I came upon the city and the king hired me on as court magician. Happy now? I can I go back to sleep?"

"No." Narda answered, "What did the portal guardian want in return for letting you through?"

"He said if I should happen across a way to empty out the city, I could do him a favour by doing so." the man answered, "I did not ask why. I found the curse and the herbs to avoid the curse. The herbs caused these bubbles and I had to hurry to cast the curse before anyone saw me and saw the bubbles. Since casting the curse I have been exhausted and just want to be left alone to sleep."

"We can not let you sleep." Narda said, "Not until you lift the curse."

"I do not know how to lift the curse," the man said.

"Then you have to come back with us," Narda said. She grabbed him under one arm and tried to pull him to his feet. Laken came over and took the other arm. Between them, Nard and Laken got the man to his feet. The man swayed and tried to lie back down, but did not have the energy to fight them. Narda and Laken marched the man to the edge of the forest that Narda through might be the right direction to take them back to the city. The path opened up before them. Parisa and Ely followed behind.

They walked like that until Narda and Laken got tired of holding the man up. Then Ely took the job of encouraging the man to walk with them. This path was the same as the rest of the paths they had walked since meeting the elven king, but this time Narda did not care about the surroundings. Her attention was only on the man and making sure that he kept moving. The man mumbled as he walked. Most of it was his complaining that he just wanted to sleep. The occasional one was a complaint about the bubbles that were still coming out of his mouth. Any others were too hard to hear and Narda was not that interested in listening.

Something white caught Narda's attention. She looked into the trees and she saw a white wolf, but the wolf had a transparent quality to it. Narda blinked at it and she suddenly felt like she was looking at it with two pairs of eyes. She blinked again and the feeling was gone. She glanced around, but everyone else's attention was focused on the man. Narda looked back at the white wolf. It looked back at her with bright blue eyes. Then it turned around and was gone. Narda stared at the spot where it disappeared for a second longer before her attention was brought back to the man by his mumblings.

The path ended exactly where the path they had entered the forest began. They exited the forest at a spot to be standing in the field with the city in sight. Narda almost sighed with relief, but they had already stopped too long and the man was starting to sink to his knees. Ely poked the man in the back and the man straightened up. The group started moving again. Based on the progress of the sun it was early evening and Narda wanted to get to the castle's protection before the sun went down.

As they went across the field to the gate, Narda noticed crows circling above the gate. She wondered if they were picking at the corpses of the lizard men. As they got closer, she could make out three black shapes lying in the shade of the wall. She might have thought them to be corpses, but there was an occasional movement of a tail or head.

"Trouble ahead," Narda said as she took out her bow. Parisa and Laken looked toward the gate and saw the black shapes and the crows.

"He must be using the crows as messengers this time," Parisa said, "since the last few times we have managed to kill his messengers."

"I will see what I can do about the crows." Narda said, "You and Laken deal with the hellcats. Ely, you keep an eye on the court magician."

Ely made an informative noise as the other two took

out their weapons.

They group continued closer in that formation. By the time the first crow was within range, Narda could see that the black shapes were hellcats and that they were waiting in the shadow of the wall for the group. The hellcats had gotten to their feet, but did not move out of the shadows to attack the group.

Narda shot at the closest crow. The crows were not paying much attention to the group and the crow did not dodge out of the way. The arrow went through it and the crow fell to the ground not far from where Narda was standing. She went over and pulled the arrow out. The hellcats hissed and snarled, but did not move out of the shadow.

Narda notched the arrow and shot at another crow, but this time the crows above her were paying attention. The arrow missed the crow Narda was aiming at, but it struck the crow above that one. The crow fell out of the sky, but it fell into the area of shadow where the hellcats were.

Before Narda could notched another arrow as group of crows dive bombed her. She ducked and covered her head with her arms. When the last crow had gone passed, Narda straightened up, notched an arrow, and aimed at the crow that was leading the charge at her. The arrow flew right at the crow. The crow dodged at the last moment and the next crow was hit with the arrow causing that crow to fall from the sky.

Narda had just enough time to duck and cover her head with her arms. The crows dove again. This time Narda felt the heat crackle of flame and a second later felt the ash from the dead crows. Where she could, Narda lifted her arms and looked at Ely. He was standing over the unconscious form of the man and had breathed fire on the group attacking Narda. He was also defending the man from the attacking crows. Parisa and Laken were attacking the hellcats at the edge of the shadow. They were using the hellcat's avoidance of coming into the light to their advantage.

Narda turned her attention back to the crows. She notched and aimed another arrow at the group of crows that were gathering to dive at her again. She let the arrow go. It hit two crows before bringing them down to the ground. Since the body of the one with the arrow in it was close by Narda went to it and took the arrow before firing it again. This time it only took out one.

Then Narda had to duck to avoid the diving crows. This time she hit the dirt and the heat of the flame from Ely was not as hot on her skin. Before the ash started down, Narda had rolled back to her feet and was notching another arrow. She aimed the arrow at the group of crows and fired it. The arrow hit the leader of the group that was gathering to attack her again.

There was a smaller group that dived at her this time. She ducked and covered her head with her arms. This time the crows were able to finish their dive. Narda glanced through her arms at Ely and saw that he was having his own problems with crows.

The remaining crows had split into two groups and one was attacking Narda, while the other was attacking Ely. The man had woken up and was trying to avoid being hit by the crows. Narda saw him try a spell, but he did not have enough energy for it to work. After that the man just curled up into a ball under Ely and made himself as small as possible.

Narda notched another arrow, aimed it at the group

of crows, and fired. The crow landed nearby and she pulled the arrow out and used it for the next shot. Then she ducked to get away from the diving crows before picking up the arrow again to shoot it. Narda kept doing this as the number of crows diminished.

Ely burned up large groups of crows, but ended up resorting to ripping them out of the air and crushing them. When Narda had dealt with the last crow diving at her, she started shooting at the ones bothering Ely.

When there were only three crows left, they started to fly off. Narda got two of them, but missed the third one.

"He will tell the portal guardian what happened," Narda said as she started to pull arrows out of crows, clean them off and put them away.

"Why were they attacking me?" the man asked, "I did everything the portal guardian asked me to. He would not want me to be harmed."

"But he might want you away from us," Narda said, "because we intend for you to lift the curse and he does not want that."

Parisa and Laken had finished dealing the hellcats and had joined them. Parisa started helping Narda gather arrows.

"But I told you," the man said, "I do not know how to lift the curse."

"But you will lift the curse," Narda said, "because I am not interested in going all this way to get you if you did not lift the curse."

"I do not think you have any say in the matter of whether I can or can not lift the curse," the man said

"You will lift the curse," Laken grabbed the man by his collar and pulled him down to be face to face with

Laken, "because that curse is in the way of me getting home and if you can not lift the curse we will try lifting the curse the other way. Then you will not be going anywhere, except six feet into the ground."

The man gulped, but did not respond. Laken let go of the man's collar and pushed him away. The man fell backward on to his backside.

"Let us go." Narda said, "It is getting too close to dark for my liking and we still have to get to the castle."

Narda and Parisa took the lead as Laken and Ely prodded the man forward. They went through the gates and found nothing inside attacked them. Narda, Parisa and Laken all had their weapons out and at ready as they moved forward up the street.

As they went up the street, the group was on the lookout for any more of the portal guardian's minions, but aside from a few crows that Narda picked off, they did not see any.

"It is quiet," Parisa whispered as they came near the end of the street.

"So, what is up ahead to attack us and take us out?" Narda asked.

They reached the end of the street and started along the path up to the castle. Nothing came out at them and they did not see any more crows. The group reached the part of the path that was only a short ways from the door to the castle where it leveled out. The castle looked exactly as they had left it. One door was open and the other was closed. Darla came into view through the door that was open.

"Finally, you are back," Darla called as she looked relieved to see them.

"Sorry, that it took us so long," Narda called back.

"You are not safe yet," a male voice boomed. It sounded like the portal guardian. Narda and the group stopped where they were a looked around.

"He can not be here." Darla called, "He is tied to the portal."

As if to mock those words, the portal guardian flickered into existence between Narda and the group and the door to the castle. He was twelve feet high, built up muscles, blue skin with red markings painted on, a black cloak, purple hair, and swinging a halberd that glowed faintly in the darkening sky.

"He looks like he found a way around that," Narda yelled.

"Oh no," the court magician groaned and looked like he was ready to make a run for it. Instead of running, he collapsed and curled up into a ball like he did with the crows. Narda suppressed a sigh before turning back to the portal guardian. The portal guardian laughed.

"Go," Narda said, "while he is distracted."

She notched and arrow, while Parisa and Laken gripped their swords and readied a charge. As she let loose the arrow they charged. The arrow hit the portal guardian in the chest, but instead of going in or bouncing off the arrow went right through him as he was not there. Parisa's short sword and the Wizard Slayer also went right through the portal guardian.

"He is an illusion," Darla shouted.

Narda was going to shout a question back when the portal guardian raised his halberd and swung it. He hit Parisa and sent her flying. She landed half way down the hill to the street below.

"Illusions can not hit back," Narda called to Darla.

"I will see if I can find anything while you keep him distracted," Darla shouted.

The portal guardian laughed.

"Nothing can stop me," the portal guardian boomed.

Narda ignored the portal guardian and headed down the hill to where Parisa had not moved. Parisa's eyes were open and she was blinking as if she was not sure how she ended up where she was. Narda knelt down beside her.

"Are you okay?" Narda asked.

"Winded," Parisa breathed the word out as if it took effort.

"Darla is looking for a way to stop him if we can distract him for long enough." Narda said, "Can you help, or do you have to sit this one out?"

"You need me." Parisa said, "I will be up in a moment."

"Okay," Nada said. She got up and headed back up the hill, leaving Parisa to come when she was ready.

Laken was dodging the portal guardian's halberd while still trying to do damage with the Wizard Slayer. Narda realized that Laken was doing that because he was not sure what else to do. The sword was just going through the portal guardian as if he was an illusion, but the marks he was leaving in the ground were real. How do you fight that kind of monster?

Narda looked around for Ely. She found him lying on the grass near the foot of the portal guardian. At first glance Narda thought he was trying to sneak passed the portal guardian, but then she realized that he was rubbing his stomach on the grass. Ely reached one claw out and touched the portal guardian's foot. The image of the portal guardian flickered.

Laken stepped back to see what happened, but he could not identify what happened. The portal guardian did not seem to notice that anything had happened, but he had noticed that Laken had stopped moving. Narda ran the rest of the way to Laken and pushed him so that they both went forward. The blade of the portal guardian's halberd missed them by a small amount. Laken suddenly realized how close they had been as he pulled himself to his feet. He grabbed Nada's hand and pulled them both a safe distance away from the portal guardian.

Parisa came up the hill as they backed away.

"What do we do now?" Parisa asked, "We can not do it any harm and it can take us out without trying."

"There has to be some way that we can distract it without getting ourselves killed," Narda said.

"We could run." Laken said, "Make it chase us."

"Run where?" Narda asked, "We are in the middle of a city, whose residents we want help from if we can survive this. I do not think they would appreciate the city being destroyed, especially since many of the residents are in there and breakable."

"Nothing you can do will defeat me." the portal guardian laughed again, "Your planning is useless. Why not come and fight?"

"We need to give Darla some time," Narda said.

"Talk to him." Parisa said, "Ask him questions."

"Like what?" Narda asked.

"Why can nothing defeat him?" Parisa suggested. Narda turned toward the portal guardian.

"Why can nothing we do defeat you?" Narda called up to him.

"Because I am invincible," the portal guardian

answered.

"No, you are an illusion." Narda said, "A powerful one, but still an illusion. That in not a reason why we can not defeat you."

"Illusions can not cause the damage my weapon has been causing," the portal guardian said, "or my foot."

Ely was reaching out to touch the portal guardian again, when the portal guardian lifted his foot and kicked Ely away from him. Ely rolled down the hill a little ways. Narda noticed that the portal guardian put his foot down exactly where it had been prior to lifting it. She turned back to Parisa and Laken.

"I did not think he can move from that spot," Narda said as she got the group to move a little farther down the hill.

"Why do you think that?" Laken asked.

"We are out of his weapon's reach." Narda answered, "Watch." Narda turned back to the portal guardian.

"Perhaps it is a piece added to the illusion spell that makes you able to damage things while still being an illusion." Narda said, "Or maybe you are not a good as you think you are. None of the people you have hit are badly hurt." Narda gestured to where Ely was getting up.

"Why did you not come here, Girl," the portal guardian said, "and find out how much damage I can do?"

"If you want to do damage to me, you have to come here." Narda called back, "I am not foolish enough to go to you."

"But what you want is inside the castle." the portal guardian said, "You would not want to get further away from your target when you are so close."

"He can not move," Laken said from his place behind Narda.

"If you are talking that direction," Narda called, "why not tell us how to get you out of the way."

"I am not that foolish, Girl," the portal guardian responded.

"My name is not girl," Narda said, "it is Nava. I told you that when you let us in."

"You are hardly worth remembering," the portal guardian said.

"Then why are you even here?" Narda asked.

"Because someone has been messing with things and by all reports it is you and your company." the portal guardian answered, "I figured that I might as well deal with the minor annoyance that you are before things get out of hand."

"Like we defeat you," Narda said.

"I told you," the portal guardian said, "I can not be defeated."

"I do not believe that." Narda said, "Just because you can produce an illusion of yourself does not mean you are invincible. We will find a way to defeat you and we will find a way to get rid of this illusion."

The portal guardian laughed.

"You do not even know what you have stumbled into," the portal guardian said, "and you will be dead before you find out."

Narda saw Darla come back into the door way of the castle. She had a book open in front of her. Darla stepped outside the door of the castle before looking down at the book. Narda saw her mouth move, but could not hear what she was saying. Darla then threw something in the air before saying something more.

There was a flash of lightening that hit the portal guardian. Then the lightening was gone. It did not appear to do any damage to the portal guardian.

"And what was that suppose to do?" the portal guardian laughed, "Tickle me?"

"Attack him," Darla shouted before closing the spell book and hurrying back inside.

As Narda notched an arrow, Ely let loose a jet of flame. The flame burned the portal guardian's leg and made his cloak catch on fire. Narda let loose the arrow and it hit the portal guardian in the chest. This time it stuck there. The portal guardian screamed in pain. While he was still distracted, Parisa and Laken charged him.

Narda fired off several more arrows and Parisa and Laken slashed at the portal guardian. Ely did his part with his fire. The portal guardian tried to swipe at Parisa and Laken with his halberd, but was having difficulties.

The portal guardian fell to his knees. He was hurt badly and he was in a lot of pain. Narda, Parisa, Laken, and Ely kept attacking him. The portal guardian finally toppled forward and lay still. Everyone stood there and waited for something more to happen. Nothing did for a moment and then the body of the portal guardian disappeared. The arrows Narda had put in him fell the short distance to the ground.

"Did we kill the portal guardian?" Laken asked Darla, who was coming out of the castle.

"No." Darla answered, "You killed his illusion. I made his illusion solid so that you could fight it and get rid of it, but it did nothing to the portal guardian himself, except drain some of his power."

"That is a starting point." Narda said as she collected her arrows, "The next thing we need to do is to get the court magician to lift the curse on this city."

"Where did the court magician go?" Parisa asked looking around.

"Follow the trail of bubbles," Narda said pointing to a group of bubbles that were floating skyward from somewhere down the hill.

Laken and Ely headed down the hill to fetch the court magician.

"Why could he not lift the curse from where you found him?" Darla asked, "We have been waiting here expecting something to happen."

"He says that he can not remember how." Narda answered, "So, we brought him here so that he could read from the book. The bubbles are apparently from the herbs he had taken to prevent to curse from touching him."

"If he messed up the herbs enough for that kind of effect, how did he manage to do the curse?" Darla asked.

"I do not know." Narda answered, "But he better be able to lift the curse."

"If he does not manage to mess that up somehow as well," Darla said.

Ely and Laken came up the hill with the court magician struggling to keep up with them because they were not letting him rest.

"I will go up and get the book," Darla said. She went inside the castle. Laken and Ely marched the court magician inside and Narda and Parisa followed them. The children were sitting in the corner with the blankets and they were quiet. Laken and Ely took the court magician closer to the throne, where there was a little bit of space. Parisa went over to sit with the children. Narda followed Laken and Ely. Ely had shrunk so that he was not too big for the space. Narda looked at the statues as she passed and hoped that this would all work out.

# LIFTING THE CURSE AND GOING UP AGAINST THE PORTAL GUARDIAN FOR THE SECOND AND FINAL TIME

When Darla came back into the throne room she was carrying several books with her. She hurried over to where Narda was getting to her feet.

"Here it is," Darla said holding out a book. Narda took the book and glanced at the page it was open to. The page was the one with the curse on it. Narda turned to the court magician, who had fallen asleep sitting beside Ely. Narda kicked the court magician. He opened his eyes and blinked up at her.

"Here is it," Narda said holding the book out. The court magician reached out to take it from her, but Narda pulled it back out of his reach.

"I need it if I am supposed to lift the curse," the court magician said.

"You are going to read it off the page as I hold it." Narda said, "I already heard you mumble in your sleep about tearing the page up."

"Fine," the court magician said. Narda held out the book again and the court magician read through the page.

"Got it?" Narda asked after his eyes had gone through the whole page.

"I am still reading through it all," the court magician said. Laken pulled out the Wizard Slayer and put the point to the court magician's neck.

"You can hurry this up, or I can hurry the whole process up," Laken said.

The court magician spat out several words that sounded like magic. Narda braced herself for magical attack. Instead the statues started to glow and got brighter and brighter until Narda had to close her eyes against the light.

She opened her eyes when the light had gone down. All the statues had become living fairies that were looking at themselves and around them in confusion. The king was back to being a fairy and his old eyes looked over the room. Narda also noticed that the court magician has stopped breathing out bubbles.

The king's eyes looked Narda over and then moved to Laken, Darla and Ely. Then he looked at the group of children in the corner. The rest of the people in the throne room also realized that there were strangers and looked around. Narda felt like she should step forward and explain everything, but she was not sure what to say. She had closed the book in her hands and Laken had removed the point of the Wizard Slayer from the court magician's throat.

The fairies started muttering among themselves. It sounded more like confusion then fear. The king's eyes moved to look at the court magician, who was still on his knees. The court magician was now frozen with fear.

"You have messed with forces that you should not have touched." the king's voice was firm, "You begged to be allowed into my city and you begged to learn magic from us. We took you and we taught you magic. The magic you used to betray us."

"I am sorry," the court magician went down to his stomach and appeared to have started to cry.

"You broke our rules." the king said, "You must be punished in the appropriate manner." The king lifted his hand and pointed at the court magician. There was a small flash and the court magician disappeared to be replaced by a donkey. The donkey still had the court magician's eyes and was the same brown as his hair had been. The donkey hung its head, but did not move.

The king turned his attention to Narda.

"You and your group broke the curse," the king said, "but I see more obstacles for you."

"We need to get home." Narda said, "We were hoping that you could help us get passed the portal guardian."

"First, we must do a few things." the king said as he turned his attention back to the fairies in the throne room, "Garan, take Hallan and find him room in the stable. Nye, send word to all that we will have a banquet."

Two men closest to the throne bowed before the one left the throne room and the other put a rope around the donkey's neck before leading him out of the throne room. The king looked over the rest of the fairies standing in the throne room. Finally, he waved to dismiss them all. They bowed and shuffled out.

Parisa got up and came over to stand near Narda, but the children stayed where they were. The king looked at Darla.

"You are a mermaid," the king said.

"I am," Darla replied. She tried to bow, but her dress was too tight. "I was brought here by the collector that took over the city while you were stone. I was among the many creatures he brought here and placed in the dungeon. Narda and Parisa came and let them all out. I choose to stay and help them."

"What happened to the collector?" the king asked.

"His ashes are in the circle of fairy dust," Darla pointed to the spot on the floor. The king nodded.

"I will have that dealt with." the king said, "Do you wish to stay, or would you like to go home?"

"If you will help them get to their home, I would like to go back to mine," Darla answered.

"I will help them get home," the king said.

"Good luck," Darla said as she hugged Narda and then Parisa.

"Good bye," Narda said.

When Darla was ready, she nodded to the king. He pointed his finger at Darla and she disappeared without even a flash of light.

"Now, on to the rest of you." the king said, "The only way for you to go home is through the portal and the only way to get through the portal is passed the portal guardian, which you said you needed help with. Perhaps you can give a brief explanation why you need help with the portal guardian."

"The portal guardian was the one who asked the magician to put a curse on the city." Narda said, "He also had the collector working for him. The collector was going through the portal and kidnapping children from the city where we live. Since we have killed the collector, the portal guardian has been sending his minions to attack us and then he sent an illusion of himself to attack us."

"I see," the king said. A troubled looked crossed the king's face.

"Can you help us get home?" Narda asked.

"This is not going to be that easy," the king said, "and I will explain why. A portal guardian is not born as a portal guardian, but becomes one after defeating the previous portal guardian. The current portal guardian was a champion, who defeated the old portal guardian because he had gone insane and was having trouble distinguishing what was real and what was in his head. When the portal guardian is defeated a prophecy appears as to who will defeat the current portal guardian. The current prophecy is that a human with a powerful weapon will come through the portal to defeat the portal guardian. That would explain why the portal guardian was having the collector kidnapping children. He was looking for the human, who would defeat him. He has become more and more power hungry over these past years. That could be seen in who he has been letting through the portal.

"If I sent you all to the portal in hopes that he would let you through, he would probably try and kill all of you. And I can not just send you home from here. The portal guardian must be defeated and replaced before any of you can get home."

"I will do," Laken said as he drew himself up to his full height. He still looked like a thirteen-year-old looking for a parent to be proud of him. The king signaled for Laken to come to him. Laken stepped forward. The king placed his hand on the top of Laken's head and closed his eyes. The king opened his eyes a moment later and removed his hand.

"If you go to challenge the portal guardian, you will die." the king said, "The weapon in your hand might be the weapon of prophecy, but you are not the person to wield it."

"Then that person is me." Narda said, "I brought the sword with me when I came here to rescue the children. Parisa and I came through the portal separately from the rest. The collector did not kidnap us."

The king looked at Narda with serious eyes that suggested that she had a great choice ahead of her. He signaled her to come to him. She stepped closer to him. He placed a hand on her head as he closed his eyes. Narda felt the slight tingle of magic go through her. The king opened his eyes and lifted his hand, but did not immediately speak. Narda stepped back from the king before turning to Laken. She held out her hand and he handed her the Wizard Slayer. Narda put the sword back in its sheath at her side.

Narda looked around at the room and saw Parisa near her.

"There is something else," Narda said turning back to the king.

"What is it?" the king asked.

"Parisa has been living on the streets of city of Proster." Narda answered, "Before that she lived in an orphanage. When we came through the portal, the portal guardian said that it was strange for a fairy and a human to be a traveling together. As far as she has known all her life, Parisa is human, but she would like to know for sure whether she is human or fairy. And she would really like wings."

"We can find out," the king said with a smile. He signaled Parisa to step forward and she did. He put his hand on her head and closed his eyes. A minute past before he opened his eyes and removed his hand.

"You are a fairy." the king said, "You are a forest fairy to be precise. You must have gotten lost and when you passed through the portal into the human world your magic got locked, which is why you look human and did not have wings. I can unlock your magic if you wish."

"I would like that," Parisa said in a small voice. The king touched Parisa's temple lightly with one finger. There was a burst of fairy dust and Parisa changed from being human size to being small enough to fit in Narda's hand. She now had two clear gossamer wings. The clothes she had been wearing had been replaced with a dress sewn together from leaves. Her light brown hair fell down her back in ringlets, rather than being straight and stopping just below her chin.

Parisa opened her own eyes and looked down at herself. She immediately started giggling and flying around.

"Look at me," Parisa cried as she twirled in front of Narda before taking off to fly around the room. Narda smiled as she watched her friend. Parisa's laughing was contagious and everyone was smiling at her glee of being able to fly. The children in the corner were laughing with her.

It took five minutes before Parisa came back to stand near Narda. She changed into a grown up form. In this form she was about five feet tall with a longer skirt, but everything else was the same from when she was smaller.

"Sorry," Parisa said as she struggled to go back to being serious. She was still flexing her wings in excitement. The children had stopped laughing, but the whole room was still on the happy emotions.

"Now you know what happened to your wings," Narda said with a smile.

"Thank you," Parisa said. They hugged each other.

When they had let go of each other, Narda turned back to the king. The whole mood of the room shifted back to serious.

"I will take on the portal guardian," Narda said.

The king nodded.

"I can help you a little bit," the king said once more signaling Narda to step forward. Narda stepped forward.

"You are now ready in your heart." the king said, "I will make you ready in body." He touched his finger to the side of Narda's temple.

Images and knowledge flashed through Narda's mind. How to use a sword, how to use the Wizard Slayer, the portal guardian's weaknesses, and more practice with her bow. It was like she was living through years of training while standing there not moving. It all flashed through Narda's head very quickly, but she felt like her body had been trained to fight.

The king took his hand away from Narda's head and she was back standing in the throne room. She had changed in that moment, just as she had seen Parisa change. Narda was now sixteen, rather than fourteen.

She was taller and more muscular. She wore customized armour and had the Wizard Slayer sheathed at her side. Her brown hair was longer and braided back out of her way.

"Now you are ready to face the portal guardian," the king said. Narda nodded since she was not sure what else to say.

"You will succeed," the king said.

"I know," Narda said quietly.

"If we are going to do this, we should get going," Parisa said. Narda turned to Parisa to say something.

"You are going to need some help," Parisa said, "and now I am able to help, so there is no way you are leaving me behind." Parisa stood there looking back at Narda with her hands on her hips and a line of stubbornness across her forehead.

"Okay," Narda said giving in with a smile.

"Good," Parisa said.

Two fairies came into the throne room carrying to traveling packs.

"These are for you," the king said. Narda took one and Parisa took the other one. They shouldered them before Narda turned back to the king.

"Parisa will come back when we have defeated the portal guardian," Narda said, "and then you can send the children so that they can go home."

"We will await her," the king said.

"Thank you for all your help," Narda said before bowing to the king.

"Good luck to you," the king said.

Narda and Parisa turned and headed out of the throne room. Outside the castle the darkness of night had fallen, but the city was lit up with the lights from the windows of the buildings. Narda and Parisa looked out over the city one more time. It was a beautiful view from the top of the hill. The sky was completely dark, so the only difference between the sky and the mountains on the horizon was the stars that shone. Anything beyond the city wall was lost in darkness, but the city was visible through yellow squares of light. There were sounds of the occasional night bird, but most of the night's noises were muffled with the city's residents moving around and organizing the banquet that the king asked for. Narda wondered what they ate at such a banquet and was sorry that she would miss it.

Narda started again and Parisa followed. They walked down the hill. When they reached the street people would stop to watch them go by. None of the people said hello, or asked them questions. The only thing Narda saw was some mouthing good luck and a few that looked like they were praying for Narda and Parisa. Narda wondered what god fairies worship. Her father had always told her that there was only one and the church had backed him on that point, but did fairies believe that as well? Did they worship saints as humans did? If they did, were they the same saints, or different ones?

Narda and Parisa reached the end of the street and came to the gate. They glanced back at the city. Narda bid it farewell and Parisa looked it over one more time just in case. They turned back around and went through the gate. They continued along the path that would lead them to the forest.

They were half way between the city and the forest, when Parisa checked over her shoulder.

"Something is following us," Parisa said.

"I know." Narda said, "It is Ely."

Parisa glanced behind them again and saw Ely appear.

"Once you feed a dragon he does not leave you alone," Narda said.

"I do not remember seeing him after the court magician said the words to lift the curse," Parisa said.

"I think Ely went invisible about that point." Narda said, "Probably to avoid scaring people. The king did not seem to notice him, but maybe he just could not see him."

"Most likely he did not see any point in taking notice of him," Parisa said.

"Well, Ely is not likely to go back there for the king to bother with," Narda said.

"You are not immortal." Parisa said, "You can not be portal guardian forever."

"I do not know how being the portal guardian works." Narda said, "I just know that I have to defeat the current portal guardian so that Laken and the others can go home and I get the position. Once I have that position, I am stuck with it until someone else comes along to defeat me."

"So, I guess neither of us gets to go back to Proster," Parisa said.

"I will have to send word back with Laken." Narda said, "I do not want my father to worry about me. He will understand that I did not have any choice and that I can not come home. My parents were not sure what to do with me anyway. Now they have an heir to the throne and someone to marry off without worrying what to do with me."

"I do not think that would be a big comfort when it

comes losing a child," Parisa said.

"They do not really have much of a choice," Narda said, "because I have made mine and I can not go back on it now."

Parisa did not respond and they continued walking without speaking. Just before they reached the forest, Narda stopped and went through her travel pack. She took out a lantern and lit it before they continued. The moon was not in the sky tonight so the only light they had been walking by had been the stars and the light from the city, but in the forest it was dark. Even with the lantern there was many things that looked menacing when viewed in the light would have just been bushes and trees. There were also the rustling of various night animals. Occasionally a pair of eyes would peer out at them from beside the path.

Narda and Parisa did not draw weapons or even jump at most of the sounds coming from the forest. They could not sense any actual danger and there had not been any when they had gone through the forest to get to the city. Nothing tried to attack them and a few times the rustle was moving away from them as soon as the creature realized that they were there.

Narda and Parisa reached the part of the path that twisted and turned. With the darkness, Narda had to pay more attention to where they were going to avoid stepped off the path. Most of the stuff that they had passed on the way to the city were not visible in the dark, but when they went by the clearing with the circle of mushrooms all the mushrooms glowed as if to invite them to come into the clearing. Narda and Parisa kept walking.

They had been walking a while before they reached

the straight stretch of the path that signalled that they were getting closer to the field.

"I thought that we would only be gone for an afternoon." Parisa said, "We would just follow the collector and then go back for help. I was hoping that I could beg supper from the castle kitchen again. Then I was going to have to find a new place to sleep for the night because someone took the one I was using."

"We probably should have gone back and found someone to tell." Narda said, "But my mother had been ordering me around and making me do things that I did not want to do. All I wanted was to be treated like an adult and I figured that going after the collector would get me that."

"It has been interesting." Parisa said, "I do not have to beg for food or sleep on cold cobble stones. And I have wings. That is the greatest part. You are different now too."

"I am trained to fight the portal guardian." Narda said, "Which is not a great as having wings, but it is okay."

"Things will turn out okay." Parisa said, "You have help from me and Ely in your fight with the portal guardian. We will succeed and everyone will be all right. Being a portal guardian must be interesting at least."

"I hope so," Narda said.

When they finally reached the edge of the forest, Narda and Parisa stopped. The field was there with the grass moving in the gentle breeze. Their tracks were still visible.

"I know we should go on," Narda said, "But it had been a long day and I am tired."

"We can stop." Parisa said, "You need to be rested before you face the portal guardian."

Narda sat down on the path.

"I wonder how we are going to find him," Narda said as she searched through her pack for some food.

"Maybe we walk to where we came in and he takes us to the black space and we battle there," Parisa suggested sitting down near Narda. Ely flopped down on his belly behind them. Narda pulled out some food and started to eat.

"It is kind of disorienting to be in the black space." Narda said, "I hope wherever we end up fighting him is not as confusing."

"I guess," Parisa said.

"We will find out," Narda said.

They sat in quiet for several minutes while Narda ate and feed some to Ely. When she was finished eating, Narda lay down and closed her eyes. She was not going to sleep so much as lie down and rest for a few minutes.

*Narda opened her eyes to see trees overhead. The sky through the branches was blue and the sun was filtering through. She had slept too long. Narda sat up and looked around. Parisa and Ely were missing so was the field. In all directions was just trees and bushes, but it reminded Narda more of the forest where the elves were instead of the one she and Parisa had just gone through.*

*A white wolf slipped through the bushes to Narda's left. She looked over at it. The wolf stared back at her with its bright blue eyes.*

*"Hello," Narda said holding out her hand to the wolf. The wolf walked over to her and let her pet it*

*once before turning and heading back toward the bush. When it reached the bush, the wolf turned back to see if Narda was coming. Narda got to her feet and followed the wolf.*

*The wolf led her through the bushes, through the throne room of the fairy castle, through a clearing with a swirling portal of silver and blue, through a room that looked like Narda's room at home, and through a field. The wolf led the way to a circle of trees. Narda could not see what was in the circle because the trees were too close together, but the wolf managed to squeeze through. Narda followed the wolf and found the way opened for her. She found herself sitting on the bed in the clearing with the tent overhead and Kathan sitting on the other bed. The white wolf was nowhere in sight.*

*"You have changed," Kathan said as his indigo eyes looked her over.*

*"I had to." Narda said, "I had to become a warrior to fight the battle with the portal guardian. The fairy king helped me. I need to get back there. I need to finish this." Narda started to get up. Kathan put his hand on her arm. It felt warm and Narda sat back down. Kathan withdrew his hand.*

*"You are already there." Kathan said, "You are just sleeping."*

*"Then I need to wake up." Narda said, "How can you feel so real if I am sleeping?"*

*"You will understand," Kathan said with a smile. He disappeared slowly. Narda could still feel his presence even after he was gone.*

Narda opened her eyes to see that the sky was dark

blue and there were streaks of pink through it. The lantern was sitting beside her, but the flame had been put out. She realized that she was a little cold, but lying next to something warm. The something warm was also breathing. Narda slowly sat up being careful not to disturb Ely. She looked around. Parisa was still sitting in the same place she was when Narda went to sleep.

"I did not mean to actually fall asleep," Narda said.

"It is okay." Parisa said, "You only slept a couple hours and you obviously needed it." Narda put the lantern back in her travel pack.

"I guess we should be going," Narda said as she stood. Ely uncurled from his sleeping position.

"Okay," Parisa said as she got up.

Narda and Parisa started across the field with Ely following behind them. It was an easy walk across the field. The trail that they had left was clear. There was more than enough light that they could see by. None of the portal guardian's minions had been seen since before the curse had been lifted. Once she was moving Narda warmed up. It felt like a good day for a walk and Narda enjoyed it especially without the thought of what was at the end of it.

Narda did notice that when they entered the field and left the forest they left behind any sounds of animals and birds. The field was lifeless, except for the wind moving the grass. It was quiet without the sound of animals moving. The wind was soundless as it went by. It was unnerving in a way and made Narda wonder if the grass was an illusion, or if the field had an origin that would cause such a quiet.

Narda, Parisa and Ely reached the point of which Narda and Parisa had entered the field. They looked around, but there was nothing there that would indict what they should do next. A crow appeared overhead and started crying at them. Narda took out her bow and notched an arrow. The crow continued to circle them and make noise. Narda fired at the crow and the arrow hit it causing it to fall from the sky and land several feet to the group's left. Narda, Parisa and Ely stood there and waited to see if anything would happen, but nothing did.

"We are trying to get home." Narda called out, "This is where we entered so this is where we should be able to exit. Let us exit the portal."

"You do not command me," the portal guardian's voice boomed from everywhere around them.

"Open the portal and we will go home," Narda called.

"You have no authority over me," the portal guardian responded.

"I am the daughter of King Proster." Narda shouted in a commanding voice, "You will let us go home."

The portal guardian appeared in the field near them. He looked the same as the illusion, except that he was only eight feet tall with his halberd the correct size for that height and nothing glowed. He slammed the bottom of his halberd on the ground.

"You are a child," the portal guardian said, "and have no authority over me."

"Shall we see?" Narda asked as she pulled out the Wizard Slayer. Ely got ready to attack and Parisa took out the sword she had, which was the exact size for her as if it had grown when she did.

"You foolish children." the portal guardian said, "You can not hope to defeat me."

"We will see," Narda said as she moved forward. Parisa and Ely fanned out to each side of Narda and also started moving forward with her.

The portal guardian pointed his halberd at the sky and lightning came down at the three points that Narda, Parisa and Ely were. Narda rolled forward. Parisa turned to her small fairy form and managed to avoid the lighting. Ely rolled to the side.

Narda charged from there. The portal guardian thrust his halberd at Narda. Narda stopped her charge to dodge out of the way. He swept the halberd in her direction and Narda ducked under it.

Ely inhaled and exhaled flame toward the portal guardian. The portal guardian moved out of the way before kicking Ely in the side. Ely rolled from the impact of the kick, but only a few feet. Then Ely was back up and headed toward the portal guardian.

Parisa had changed back to her bigger form and had gotten close enough to slash at the portal guardian's arm. She managed it twice before the portal guardian swept his halberd her direction and she had to back away to avoid being hit.

Narda swung her sword at the portal guardian and he blocked it with his halberd. She freed her sword and tried again, but he blocked that too. She swung again as she move in closer. The portal guardian blocked this swing as well.

With the portal guardian busy, Ely moved in close enough to bite him in the leg, but before he could put his jaws around the portal guardian's leg Ely was kicked. This kick caused him to reel back and pause to think about how next to attack.

Parisa moved close again to slash at the portal

guardian's arm. The portal guardian swung his halberd in an arc and caught all three of them in it. They all landed in the same pile to one side of things. Narda was the first one to her feet with her sword ready. Parisa was the next to get up, but her sword had landed closer to the portal guardian than to her. He noticed and stepped on it to push it into the ground. Parisa ignored the sword and changed back to be small.

Ely lay there stunned for a couple minutes before rolling back on to his feet. He unfolded his wings and gave them an experimental flap before using them to get airborne.

Narda reached the portal guardian first and he brought his halberd down on her sword before she could swing it. Narda kept a grip on her sword as she freed it from the halberd. She brought her sword down on the halberd before the portal guardian could pull it back. The vibration went up the halberd, but the portal guardian kept his grip on it. Narda felt a charge build in the halberd and quickly dodged out of the way. Out of the end of the halberd came a crow that was three feet in wingspan and glowing purple.

The crow immediately headed for Ely. Ely saw it coming and shot fire at it. The crow dodged that and headed into a dive toward Ely, gleaming beak first. Ely did not get out of the way fast enough and the crow slashed his side. Ely did slap the crow with his tail as it flew passed. This knocked the crow a ways and it took a moment to right itself. The crow headed back toward Ely.

Parisa flew to the air above the portal guardian's head and showered him in fairy dust. The portal guardian's eyes grew heavy with sleep for one brief moment. He shook the fairy dust off and swatted at Parisa. Parisa dodged the portal guardian's hand several times before he hit her. Parisa was half way to the ground before she righted herself and headed back to the air over his head.

Narda was attacking and blocking the portal guardian's halberd, which he could wield without paying full attention to it. She was starting to get frustrated and hitting the halberd with more force, but it was not doing her much good. The halberd did not seem to be taking any damage to it, just as the Wizard Slayer had not taken any damage. Narda thought that the halberd might be a power source for the portal guardian, which meant that if she could get him to lose the halberd he would be easier to defeat. Narda continued to block and attack the halberd, but she tried to have her attacks hit farther down the halberd to where the portal guardian's grip was on it.

The crow dived at Ely again. Ely dodged at the last second and the crow missed him. The crow took some space to turn around and dive again. Ely dodged the attack and once again slapped the crow with his tail. The crow had gone down farther this time and just about missed being hit with the tail, but Ely's tail had connected with the crow. The crow did a couple rolls before straightening out. The crow came back at Ely. The crow's black eye gleamed with an idea for its next attack. Ely flapped his wings and waited in one place for the crow to get there. The crow dived again, but before the crow could reach his side, Ely put his claw out and scrapped his claws across the crow's underside. The crow broke off his attack and flew far enough away from Ely to avoid being attacked again. Ely did not wait this time, but flew after the crow. The crow did not realize that Ely had followed it until it had started to turn around and try another attack. The crow turned back around and tried to get as far from Ely that it could dive again. Ely closed in on the crow before exhaling the flames. The flames hit the crow and the ashes tumbled to the ground. Ely headed back towards the battle with the portal guardian.

Parisa had gotten above the portal guardian's head again without him swatting her. She proceeded to dust him again, but this time she used sneezing powder rather than sleeping powder. The portal guardian tried shaking this powder off too, but Parisa kept dusting him in it. The portal guardian started to sneeze. Narda took advantage of this and started attacking the arm that held the halberd. She got three good slashes before the portal guardian gained control over himself again and blocked her. The portal guardian shook himself again to be rid of the dust.

Narda swung again and was blocked by the portal guardian's halberd. She felt a charge build in the halberd again. She got her sword free and backed away from the halberd. This time a semitransparent giant hand came out of the end of the halberd and started toward Narda.

Parisa was still showering the portal guardian with the sneezing dust in an attempt to keep him distracted enough that Narda could do some damage. She did not notice when the portal guardian brought his halberd up and swung it at her. The halberd caught Parisa in the side and sent her crashing into the ground some distance away.

Narda saw Parisa crash and saw that Parisa was not

getting up, but Narda could not run to help her or see if she was still alive. The hand continued to move toward Narda. Narda had backed off several steps before she had seen Parisa hit. But this time, rather than back off Narda took a firmer grip of the Wizard Slayer and swung it so that it sliced through the giant hand. The hand vanished in two puffs of smoke. Narda started toward the portal guardian again. The portal guardian brought the halberd back down to stop her. Narda brought the Wizard Slayer down on the halberd with as much force as she could manage. This caused not only vibration to go down the halberd, but also a white light. The light flowed over the halberd and its appearance changed. Rather than the gleaming gold and silver weapon, it became a steel and wood. The white light stopped at the portal guardian. Narda was not sure whether that was because the sword's abilities did not go that far or there was nothing magical about the portal guardian's appearance.

The portal guardian cursed and freed his weapon before swinging it at Narda. Narda brought up the Wizard Slayer to block the halberd. She freed her sword quickly and struck the halberd again. That strike did some damage to the halberd and the whole thing vibrated again. Narda moved in closer as she raised her sword again. This time she caught the portal guardian's wrist as well as the wooden part of the halberd. The portal guardian dropped the halberd.

Ely had circled around behind the portal guardian without being noticed. He had landed right behind the portal guardian and inhaled. He exhaled the flame just as the portal guardian dropped the halberd and caught the portal guardian at the knees. The portal guardian screamed in pain as he fell forward on to his knees.

Narda had raised her sword again and swung it at the portal guardian's neck. The portal guardian did not have time to raise his arm to stop the sword before it reached his head. The Wizard Slayer sliced clean through the portal guardian's neck causing both head and body to collapse to the ground.

Narda had jumped back to avoid being hit by the body. Ely exhaled flame on to the body causing some burns and the cloak to catch on fire. Narda did not stay to watch. She sheathed the Wizard Slayer and ran to where Parisa had fallen. She found Parisa lying on her back in the grass. Parisa had a cut on the side of her head that was bleeding, but she was breathing. There were other bruises along Parisa's side from being hit with the halberd and a few from hitting the ground.

Narda went through her travel pack and took out the first aid kit. She carefully wiped off and bandaged the wound of Parisa's head. She gently checked for any broken bones, but she relieved when she did not find any. She finished with taking care of Parisa when she noticed that her hands started to glow. Narda looked down and saw that her whole body had started to glow. The glow was getting brighter until she did not need to look down to know that she was glowing.

Narda looked back at where the portal guardian's body had fallen. It was burning, but the grass around it was resisting the flames. Ely was watching the fire, but he was not glowing. Narda felt like something within her was changing. She felt dizzy and light headed. The world started to move in ways that was not possible. Narda closed her eyes and fainted.

# NARDA BECOMES THE PORTAL GUARDIAN AND SHE SENDS THE CHILDREN BACK

Narda woke up, but did not immediately open her eyes. She was lying on something soft that was definitely not the grass that had covered the field. There were sounds here. She recognized the sound of a fireplace, water flowing, and the swish of fabric going over a stone floor. There was the strong smell of wood smoke and wine.

Narda slowly opened her eyes. She was in a room built with stones that looked like it might be part of a castle. She was lying on a velvet blanket that covered a bed. There was a fireplace to her left with a table on the other side of it from her. On the table was a bottle of wine. To Narda's right was a doorway with a garden visible through it. And the sound of the fabric came from a woman pacing across the small space of the room. The woman was dressed in a blood red dress that had lots of flowing fabric, but a low neckline that looked like she could spill out of at any moment. Her black hair was up in a fancy way with ribbons that matched her dress weaved through it. She was holding a goblet in her hand and would take a sip out of it occasionally.

"Where am I?" Narda asked. The woman twirled towards Narda. Narda saw that she had emerald eyes that appeared to hold no emotion. Her cheek bones and smooth forehead made her appear ageless and emotionless. But her red painted lips were set in a line of frustration.

"That does not matter." the woman's voice was harsh, "You will never return here ever again. You are only here because it is dictated that all new portal guardians must be briefed on their duties. However, most come here awake. Your sleeping has pushed back my very busy schedule."

"I am sorry," Narda said as she sat up. The woman's mouth gave a little bit, but still looked slightly annoyed.

"We have never had a human guardian for the portal." the woman said, "No human has ever been able to defeat the guardian. Your coming was predicted, but you came earlier than predicted. You should not have come for several more years. Fortunately, the fairy king helped us by aging you to a more appropriate time in your life. You are now guardian of the portal for which you defeated the previous guardian. Your powers are controlling of the portal and who is able to come through it in either direction. You are charged with keeping trouble out of the human realm and keeping trouble out of the magic realm. You can not leave the portal unguarded no matter what. You may keep your dragon companion with you. You will live in the area built for guardians near the portal. You may have visitors, but no one can live there for an extended period of time because it will have adverse effects on them. Also, and finally, if you feel it is necessary you may close the portal and open it only when you choose. Any questions?"

"I am human," Narda said, "and that means that I am mortal. What happens when I die?"

"As guardian you are no longer mortal." the woman said, "You will die when it is time for the next guardian and that will be in battle against them."

"Who will be the next guardian?" Narda asked. The woman did not answer immediately, but her eyes went white and a male voice came out of her mouth.

"The guardianship will be passed not through battle as all say, but through inheritance when the being is aged to understanding."

Before Narda could ask any more questions the room was gone and she was standing in front of a hut with three wells next to it. There was nothing else in the space. It was light, but there was nothing around. Even the path she stood on did not have any colour, texture, or shape, but it was solid. The hut was made out of wood and had a door and two windows. Narda walked over and opened the door. Inside was a large entrance way that was twice the width of the outside of the hut and had a large staircase that went up to a second storey. There was also another doorway off to the left of the entrance way. Narda stepped inside. It was all made with wood and painted in shades of purple and gold. Narda went over to the doorway and looked inside. It appeared to be a place for an animal to sleep and was big enough that Ely could lie down and be comfortable once he was full grown.

Up the stairs Narda found a bed chamber, a sitting room, a library and an exercise room. All of them had been done in the purple and gold colouring. The bedroom was large with a huge bed, a separate room for clothing, a full length mirror as well as a vanity, and a comfortable chair. There was also a separate room off it for bathing. The sitting room had matching chairs sitting around a table that was the right height for a person to sit in the chairs and play a game on the table. There were also smaller tables near some chairs with lamps on them. There was a window in this room. Narda went a looked through it. The view was that of looking through the window that was on the outside of the hut. The library's walls were completely covered with shelves and then there were shelves in rows along the floor. There no chairs to sit and read and the only lamp was one that could be taken off the wall and carried to where the light was wanted. The exercise room had equipment sitting in piles that one would use to practice their fighting skills. Along a couple of the walls were mirrors so that a person could watch themselves and check their form. The other window was in this room.

Narda left the exercise room and went down the stairs. She exited the hut through the door. She walked over to the wells that were beside the house. All three had water close to the top of them. The first one had an image in it. The image was of the clearing in the forest where Narda and Parisa had found the portal when they followed the collector from Proster. The second one was just silver and blue swirls. The third one showed the image of the field where she, Parisa and Ely had battled the previous portal guardian. In this one, Narda could see Parisa sitting up in her bigger size and Ely lying beside her.

Instinctively Narda touched the water and wished herself back in the field. She appeared in the field without any feeling of having moved.

"Narda," Parisa called as she struggled to get to her feet. Ely looked up and was on his feet in no time. Both looked very happy to see her. Narda went over to them.

"What happened?" Parisa asked.

"I am the new portal guardian," Narda said, "with all the power that entails."

"And?" Parisa asked.

"It comes with responsibilities and a hut." Narda answered, "I was told that Ely could live with me and other people could visit me, but bad things happen to people who stay for a long time."

"We won." Parisa said, "The portal guardian is dead, you are the new portal guardian, and we can get the children back home."

"We won," Narda said with a smile.

"I have to get back to the fairy city, but I still feel woozy," Parisa said. Narda reached out and took Parisa hand. She held Parisa's hand in both of hers and a warm glow went up Parisa's arm and into her body. The warm glow enveloped her before disappearing. Parisa had more colour in her face, but the bruises were still visible.

"Apparently, it does not heal you all the way," Narda said, "but I am discovering my powers more by a little voice that says I can do things then my knowing myself what I can do."

"I feel much better." Parisa said, "Being a portal guardian is almost as good as being a fairy."

"Except that you can go anywhere you want." Narda said, "I can only go to three places."

"Powers are still great?" Parisa asked.

"Powers are still great," Narda answered with a smile.

"I will go back and get the children," Parisa said, "and then I want to see this hut that you have."

"You will not believe it," Narda said.

"I will be back as soon as I can," Parisa said. Parisa got to her feet and changed into her smaller form. She flew back to where the path was that would take her through the forest.

Narda turned to Ely.

"Want to see your new home?" Narda asked. Ely nodded. Narda thought of her and Ely being in the place where the hut was.

They were standing in front of the hut with Ely looking around as if trying to figure out how he got there.

"Here is our new home," Narda said as she opened the door. Ely had to get smaller to go through the doorway.

"And over here is your room," Narda said going to the doorway on left. Ely followed her and peered inside the room. He looked it over before stepping inside. He went back to his normal form and found that he could move freely in the space. There was also a door on the other side of the room that he could open and go outside the hut. Ely turned around to make sure that he had not missed anything in inspecting the room before flopping down on his side and relaxing.

"I am glad you are happy," Narda told Ely. She left him and went back outside the hut. She went over to the wells, but found nothing in the images yet. Narda watched for a few minutes, but she was starting to get tired. She went back into the hut and went up to the library. She went to the first shelf and looked over the titles. There was a book of fables that looked interesting so Narda took it and went back to the wells. She read as she waited for Parisa to come back with the children.

It seemed to Narda that only an hour or so past when she saw Parisa bring the children into the field. She set the book down on the path beside the wells and thought herself down to the field.

"Oh good." Parisa said, "I was not sure whether I should yell or not."

"I was watching for you," Narda said.

"So, you are now the portal guardian." Laken said, "What should I tell your father?"

"Tell him that due to things beyond my control I will not be coming home." Narda answered, "Tell him that I love him and that I am sorry."

"Okay," Laken said with a nod.

"When I take you through the portal you will have to find your way out of the forest and back into town," Narda said.

"The king gave us what we need to travel back to the city," Laken said. Narda now noticed the travel packs that each child carried.

"I drew a map of what I remembered of our journey to the portal," Parisa said.

"I hope that all helps you find your way home," Narda said.

"We will be okay," Laken said.

Narda thought of the group of children to be in the clearing on the other side of the portal. The children disappeared. Narda thought of her and Parisa back on the path outside the hut.

They were now standing there.

"Amazing." Parisa said as she looked around, "Not much here though."

"I think this space was built just to give the portal guardian some place to live," Narda said.

"I thought you would get more than just a hut to live in," Parisa said, "especially after everything you had to go through to get it."

"I do not find it too bad." Narda said as she went to the door, "Ely likes his room."

"Room?" Parisa asked, "There is more than one room?"

Narda opened the door and gestured for Parisa to enter. Parisa did and stopped immediately. She looked around in awe.

"That is Ely's room on the left," Narda said.

"What about on the right?" Parisa asked. Narda entered behind Parisa and moved around her. There was a doorway on the right side of the entrance way.

"I do not know." Narda answered, "It was not there before."

"Let us check it out," Parisa said.

They went to the doorway on the right. Inside was a bedroom. The room was painted pink with white trim. There was a bed with a gaze curtain around it. There was a vanity, a comfortable chair and two separate rooms off it, one was full of clothing and the other was for bathing.

"I guess when I have guests the hut provides a

bedroom for them," Narda said.

"If this is my room to stay in, what does yours look like?" Parisa asked as she stood in the centre of the room and kept spinning to see everything at once. Her eyes were lit up and she would giggle at something she saw.

"Not quite as pink," Narda answered. She sat down in the chair and let Parisa just take in the bedroom.

"This is the most amazing room ever." Parisa exclaimed when she finally had to sit down on the floor because she had gotten too dizzy from spinning, "What else is there in this hut?"

"A library, a sitting room and an exercise room," Narda answered.

"Everything you need," Parisa said, "except a kitchen. Kitchens are necessary for living."

"I would not know what to do in a kitchen." Narda said, "Everything has been cooked for me all my life. I might burn this place down if I tried to use a kitchen."

"If there is no kitchen, how will you eat?" Parisa asked.

"Maybe being here means that I am never hungry," Narda answered.

"That maybe so, but what about any guests?" Parisa asked, "What if they get hungry? Does that affect them too? What if you want to eat something?"

"I do not know," Narda said with a shrug.

"Let us see the rest of this place," Parisa said as she got to her feet.

Narda stood up and they left the guest room. Narda took Parisa upstairs and showed her the rooms up there. In the sitting room, they found supper had been set out on one of the game tables. There were two full plates.

On one plate was chicken and potatoes covered in gravy with a slice of apple pie beside it. The other plate contained a meat pastry with a dish of strawberries next to it. Beside both plates were goblets of cider.

"Apparently they provide the food," Narda said as they sat down in the chairs. Narda sat down in front of the meat pastry and Parisa sat down in front of the chicken.

"And it looks delicious," Parisa said. They started to eat and did not talk while they did so.

"Tastes delicious too," Parisa said when they had finished eating and had sat back in their chairs to relax.

"I do not know about you, but with food in my stomach and such a long day, I am tired." Narda said, "I am going to try out my new bed." Narda got to her feet.

"See you in the morning," Parisa called as Narda head toward the door.

"See you too," Narda said. She left the library and went to the bedroom. She stripped off her clothes and left them in a heap beside the bed. Narda climbed into the bed and pulled the covers up to her neck. It felt just like her bed at home had. It was warm, comfortable and safe. Narda relaxed, but did not immediately fall asleep. Her mind went a strange place. It wondered what it would be like to have Kathan taking up the other side of the bed.

Narda closed her eyes and tried to block any more thoughts about Kathan as she tried to go to sleep. One more picture of his face appeared to her and she wondered if that was what he meant in the dream. Then she fell asleep.

Narda woke up. The level of light in the room was

enough that she could see, but made it feel like it was still night. She crawled out of bed and put on her clothes, which were folded nicely on the chair. They had been cleaned and the armour was sitting in a pile on the floor. Narda left the armour where it was and left the room. She went down the stairs and out of the hut. Something was drawing her to the wells. She walked over and looked into the first well. There was nothing there except the field. Narda moved to the third well. She looked into and saw a dozen men enter the clearing. At their head was her father. He looked exactly the same as when she last saw him, except that he had the sword from his study that he used instead of taking out the Wizard Slayer and he was wearing his armour. Narda recognized several of the men behind him as being with the castle guard.

Narda's father had stopped and looked into the portal. Suddenly Narda realized that he had not run into the children and that he was going to enter the portal to go search for them. He did not know what she had done and Laken had not been able to deliver her message to him. Almost without thinking about the consequences, Narda thought of herself standing in front of the portal in the clearing. Only then did she think about that fact that her father did not know how much she had changed, but it was too late she was already standing there looking him in the eye.

He looked surprised and started to reach for his sword, but he stopped himself before he got there. The men behind him did not and pulled out their swords.

"Nava?" Proster asked. There was wonder in his voice.

"Yes," Narda answered.

"What happened?" Proster asked. The men looked at each other in wonder, but did not put their swords away.

"I saw the man kidnap Laken," Narda answered, "and I followed him into the portal. I borrowed the Wizard Slayer from you and I was going to return it. Parisa, one of my friends from the market place went with me. We followed him into the portal and we killed him with the help of a mermaid and a dragon. We found the children and lifted the curse from the city that we found. The fairy king of the city changed me so that I was sixteen and was trained to fight. Parisa helped me battle with the being that was controlling the collector. And we found out that Parisa was a fairy with her powers blocked. She is happier in the magical world inside the portal. We sent the children back, but they must have made a wrong turn or something because you did not find them. And I can not go home." Narda not realize it, but she found that when she had rattled everything off that she was crying. She felt embarrassed and wanted to turn away. Her father just took her in his arms and held her there. She once again felt safe and just let herself cry.

"It is all right," Proster whispered to her over and over to her until she gained control over herself again. The men behind him put their swords away and shuffled out of the clearing to give Proster and Narda some privacy.

When she was under control, Narda pulled away.

"Now," Proster said, "what did you mean when you said that you could not go home?"

"It was the guardian of this portal that was controlling the collector." Narda answered, "In defeating him, I was given the job of guarding the portal against any trouble from either side."

"Was there anyone else who could have fought the guardian?" Proster asked.

"Laken volunteered," Narda said, "but other than that, not really."

"Then you took a leadership position and deserve the responsibility that has been placed on you," Proster said, "and I am proud of you for doing it. If it was the guardian that was the problem then you probably could not go home because he was in the way. You chose to fight him and take his place so that the rest of the children could come home. Also, you will be able to stop anyone else from causing trouble by going through the portal."

"I will stop it completely." Narda said, "I will close the portal."

"See, you are the right person for the position," Proster said smiling at his daughter.

"I suppose," Narda said.

"My men and I will search for the children,." Proster said, "We will find them and we will make sure that they get home."

Narda nodded and smiled a slight smile.

"As for 'borrowing' the Wizard Slayer." Proster said, "I would have preferred that you had not taken it without my permission, but it sounds like it helped you fight the battles you needed to fight. That is a good thing."

"I forgot it." Narda said, "I should get it for you."

"Keep it." Proster said, "You will need it more than I will, especially if you are closing the portal. I will also not get to leave anything to you when I die, so the Wizard Slayer can be your inheritance. I am sure that your siblings will not mind, since they will get everything else."

"I am sorry for disobeying mother." Narda said, "I did go to church, but I went up to the balcony with the other children so that I would not have to sit with her. I wanted to avoid the collector, but he was not there. When I went outside, I saw him in an alley way. I really wanted her to treat me as an adult so much that I followed him."

"I will tell her that you are sorry," Proster said, "but try not to hang on to all of that. You are an adult now and she will be proud of the woman you have become, even if she missed all of it."

"I met a forest elf," Narda said, "and he said that because your family line had dwarf in it that we all have the ability to fall in love with one person. That we have lifemates, he called it. It was something about only falling in love with one person in our lives, but because of the human blood we can have other lovers."

"I have never talked to a forest elf," Proster said, "nor do I know what all we get from our ancestors besides problems with being so short, but I do know that when I saw your mother I fell in love with her. She was the only woman I met that I fell in love with. However, your grandfather had two wives, both of which he claimed to love. The first I believe that he did love because of how many children they had together. The second one I believe that he did love her because there is no other reason in the world for him putting up with her behaviour. His first wife loved him, but his second did not. But people are weird in what they get from their parents and what they do not get from their parents. This forest elf could be right and your grandfather could be the exception. I do not have any explanation as to why I fell in love with your mother and not anyone else. Why are you asking about this?"

"Because the forest elf showed up in a dream I had," Narda answered, "and sometimes my mind will bring his image up. And whenever these things happen it makes my stomach feel funny. I have never met anyone who makes me feel like that and sometimes I do not mind and others I try very hard to push those thoughts away. I had a thought last night that with me being the guardian of the portal I wold not see him again, I felt sad. I have never met him before in my life and my life has nothing to do with his. His father wants nothing to do with humans or any outsiders."

"It is possible that he is right and that the dwarf blood means we fall in love with one person and no other," Proster said, "and what you are describing sounds like you are experiencing the first feelings of love. But it is not full blown love as I remember feeling for your mother. I remember feeling like I could not life without her and you just feel sad about missing him. That could be your age too. The other thing is that he is a forest elf and you are part dwarf, those two do not mix well in any circumstances. I know that much about elves and dwarves. But because of your human blood I guess anything is possible. You will have to find out."

"How?" Narda asked.

"If he has fallen in love with you and he is experiencing the symptoms of love he will come to you." Proster said, "He will have no choice but come to you. Maybe by then you will figure out whether what he said is true and whether you love him."

"I am not sure whether I should hope that happens

soon or hope it never happens," Narda said.

"And those are proof that you are now an adult." Proster said, "Love tends to be an adult problem. You will work it through in time."

Proster hugged his daughter again.

"I hope so," Narda said into his shoulder.

"I have to go off and search for those children," Proster said, "and you have a portal to close." Proster moved Narda so that he could look her in the eye.

"We both have adult problems to deal with." Proster said, "So, you be careful and try to be happy."

"I will try," Narda said as she tried to smile.

Proster hugged her again, this time not letting go so soon.

"I love you," Proster whispered into Narda's ear.

"I love you too," Narda whispered back. A few more tears slide down her face as she buried it into his shoulder.

They stood there for a few more minutes as if letting go would make it all real. Someone came into the clearing and cleared his throat.

"Sir," Loic voice said.

Proster let go of Narda and she took a step back.

"Good bye," Narda said.

"Good bye," Proster replied. Narda thought herself back to the path with the huts. She looked down into the well and saw her father talk to Loic for a minute. Loic turned and left the clearing. Proster turned back around to look at the portal one last time.

"Goodbye, Father," Narda whispered to the image. Proster turned and left the clearing. Narda closed her eyes and used her power to close the portal.

# CONCLUSION?

Mitchell closed the book and studied the leather cover. It was an interesting story to read to children, or to read for the enjoyment of it. It, however, was no more real than any other book of fiction that was on his shelf. A girl left to adventure on her own. A portal between this world and a magical one. These things do not happen in the real world. This book just proved to Mitchell that his theory about one of his ancestors being a writer was likely. The first book could have been history if not for a couple elements, but this one was definitely fiction.

Mitchell stood up and took the book back to the box that was sitting on his desk. There were a lot more books to read in the box. He picked out the next one and took it back to the chair beside the fire. The maid had come in while he was reading and lit the lamps for him, but she had not added another log to the fire. It was getting late into the night and Mitchell knew that he should be headed for bed. The book in his hand called to him and begged to be read. Or maybe that sliver of doubt in the back of his head wanted this one to be as much fiction as the last one so that he knew that these were manuscripts and not some hidden history he had stumbled upon.

After setting the book on the table beside the chair, Mitchell stood up and went to the fire. He added a couple more logs to the fire. He was going to read the next book tonight and make sure that he knew beyond all doubt that these books were fiction. The government had many secrets, but Proster having this kind of history was not one of them.

# ABOUT THE AUTHOR

Heather Mantler is a lover of fairy tales and fables. She is also a student of psychology. She lives in Prince George, British Columbia. Heather is always working on another story as she hopes to finish every story idea that she has ever written down. She was a nominee for the fiction category of the 2012 Prince George Regional Arts and Cultural Awards.

Heather encourages all her readers to post their reviews on Amazon.com or Good Reads.

www.ingramcontent.com/pod-product-compliance
Lightning Source LLC
Chambersburg PA
CBHW051514170626
46811CB00002B/815

```
* 9 7 8 1 9 2 7 5 0 7 0 2 5 *
```